TALES FROM THE TEA HOUSE

A FABULOUS COLLECTION OF MARVELLOUS TALES TO TELL OR BE TOLD

CHRISTIAN WINGROVE-ROGERS

CONTENTS

ABOUT THE AUTHOR

At an early age, Christian Wingrove-Rogers suffered from an acute form of institutions allergy. It was brought on by an authoritative and traditional (as opposed to modern and forward thinking) private school and was not helped by spending Sunday mornings, that could have been spent ferally on the seashore, sitting on a hard bank badly singing dirges in a cold lightless building. The allergy was then exacerbated during a brief spell in the armed forces and later on, through various encounters with figures of authority and a draconian law designed purely to restrict the freedom of people with specific skin colour or liberal-minded attitudes. The young Christian, being a subject of the United Kingdom, which is an institution that can only exist by feeding on itself, was doomed. Therefore, in the middle of the 1980s, and in the interests of all concerned, he left...

Free from the constraints of an island mentality, he was able to look at his former homeland without dust in his eyes. What he saw there were the lies, the greed and gross perfidy of people in positions of power and respectability. Each of them being representatives of the institutions he had been told to blindly respect. This was the land he moved further away from.

Along the way and in the company of several other curious and unique fellows he travelled around most of pre-fall of wall Europe to gradually become a juggling street performer and comedian in the style of the Italian Commedia dell'arte.

Then one day while sheltering from a storm in the barn of an eighty-year-old goat herd just outside a tiny village at the end of a rough track high in the Andorran Pyrenees, Christian discovered the art and power of storytelling. The man's name was Jaketa. He had the bluest and most beautiful of eyes, eyes that could never lie, and he had never left the valley where he was born. Not even for a day.

Today after what seems like an entire lifetime, Christian still continues to perform as a juggler and comedian. But having moved from the streets and into theatres, classrooms and living rooms, it is as a storyteller that he devotes his time and energy. As well as telling Christian also teaches in schools in Africa and in Europe and has worked with the European Green Party, amongst others, giving a series of workshops teaching the art of oral storytelling. He has also turned his attention to writing the stories he tells - you have one in your hand, dear reader, and is working on a book about a poet in a garden. Currently, he writes a column on the healing power of stories for "Blickpunkt", a magazine for the Initiative Selbsthilfe Multiple Sklerose Kranker e. V.

Somebody recently asked me, upon learning that I was a professional storyteller, what it was that I did to earn a living.

It seemed to me that they were implying that the idea of being paid to tell stories was quite unimaginable. I explained that my calendar was full and that my fees were comparable to those that performers of other arts received. I also explained that I told stories not just in schools but also at festivals and board meetings of major companies. My words were being heard, but I could see that they were not sinking in. The concept of the storyteller was, to this person, a thing of the past and, particularly, childhood. Jackanory, Listen With Mother and all that.[1] Wistfully it was then remarked how it was a shame that storytelling had died out. My response was to tell a small story.

"Well then," I said after I had finished telling, "what was unimaginable or dead about that?"

Oral storytelling will never die out; the stories will make sure of that. They will always find a way to keep us thinking and questioning. Stories keep us on track. They turn up whenever we least expect them and, often, that is when we most need them.

Stories reach the hearts of the listeners who, within his or her imagination, will recognise words that resonate with them. A story is immediate. We identify with it as it unfolds in our imaginations. The storyteller works with empathy rather than logic, evoking in the listener an inner journey, a dialogue which carries a universal truth. Without visual trickery or sound effects, the story is created, co-created, purely out of words in association with the listener who has the means to perceive the values within. He or she is empowered by listening. Stories are like traditional medicine. They get to the root of where they need to get to and soothe, before problems set in.

I am still continuously amazed how the simple act of telling a story always arouses the same feelings of compassion in every listener no matter their background or age.

I have been a professional storyteller for a long time. I think I have always been a storyteller. My mother used to say that I could talk my way out of anything. My friends told me that I had a silver-speaking tongue. It seems natural to me, if I hear something extraordinary, to want to share it and stories are the most remarkable things that I know.

Storytelling is an act that causes the invisible to be seen.

The tales in this book are tales that I have told many times. They are from a repertoire of over 400 stories that I have gathered in my time as a storyteller. They are stories that have been told and retold over thousands of years by countless other storytellers from so many different countries that it is almost impossible to say with any certainty where they began their travels. Which means that they have no one single author rather they have had, and continue to have, many interpreters. Each one of whom, by transcribing and paraphrasing the tales using their unique style, has recast them for a particular audience or situation and thereby kept them alive. And relevant.

I am simply one in a long line of tellers to be doing this and surely will not be the last one. This book, apart from being meant to entertain and inform, is my way of making sure of that.

I have become aware of many of these stories through extensive reading and research. Some of the tales have been inspired by the Sufi teaching tales from the Golden Age of Persian poetry. These are stories that I love very much, and when I am telling them, my heart finds peace. Others are from Africa or the East. Almost all of the tales in this book are traditional and come from the universal and collective human spirit. Others are my work.

I wrote the story of The Field, for example, after somebody asked me to host a discussion examining the importance of storytelling, particularly in schools. I began by considering the listener rather than the teller or the tale, which is well aware of its purpose. I was interested in exploring the storyteller's role as a facilitator, as one who enhances the listeners' capability to recognise the wisdom contained within the tales. To illustrate this, I imagined a classroom to be like a field, and a farmer who sowed seed as a teacher would broadcast ideas and philosophies. The analogy, like flowers, grew and so it turned into a story.

I was inspired to call this book "Tales From The Tea House" by the thought that there are tea houses all over the world. Each society has its tea-drinking tradition and the tea house, throughout history, has been an important gathering place where people may relax and be calm. Like the stories, the tea house is no longer specific to one particular culture but all. The tea house was a perfect place, metaphorically speaking, to put one's feet up and relax, to drink some tea and listen to a tale. And just like stories, tea originated as a medicine intended to instil "calm alertness".

Please tell these stories… that is their purpose.

---

1. * Both of these were British television programs of my childhood. The latter was in black and white, of course. I am old, you know.

BY WAY OF GRATITUDE

This book was, written, edited, proofread, illustrated and generally put-together over a while by one person. That person is eternally grateful to Oliver, Silke and Nele Caspers for their ears and eyes and words. What a team they are! Their support and advice, subtle and timely as it always was, my sight clear when it was clouding and put a firmer terra under my feet.

My partner Kerstin Otto deserves plenty of "dankeschöns" for her understanding and patience as does my mother, who had to listen a lot, and the others who read the stories in their early stages and put up with numerous out of the blue e-mails. Thank you, Keith, Gabi, Ellen and Kevin.

For showing me what was possible by giving me a colossal pull up to the top of the hill to see the view, I wish to hug and thank Dr. Christine Hausmann without whom this would not have happened.

The teapot on the cover was created by Deirde Mulrooney, www.deidre-mulrooney.com.

The illustrations are my own work.

The gushing is over. "Read on, dear reader. Read on."

Christian Wingrove-Rogers Essaouira, 20.02.2020

To Dorothy

I called out to my self but my self was gone
The boundaries of my being were lost in the sea.
A wave broke and I was aware again
Of the voice that returns me to my self.

This is how it is.

The sea turns in on itself and foams
And with every foaming bit
Another being takes form.
And then, when the sea sends word
Each foaming body
Melts back into ocean's breath.

Rumi

2

TWO TRAVELLERS

This tale is well known and often told. It is both timeless and descriptive of the human condition that it could have originated anywhere in the world. It is an excellent way to begin this journey.

One ordinary late afternoon an elderly woman was working in her garden at the front of her house which happened to be the first house a traveller would come to at the end of a lane which ran into a small village. She was pulling and tugging at the weeds and stacking them neatly on the compost pile as a man came up to the garden fence. Leaning on it, he called out to her. The woman stopped her work and, hooking her little basket into the crook of her arm, went to speak to him. She could see that he had come from a long way for his shoes were dusty, and his neck scarf soaked in sweat.

"How can I help you?" She politely enquired.

"I am a stranger to these parts and intend to stay for a night in the village up ahead, but I am afraid about it because you see, I do not know how it is there. Perhaps you might tell me about it. What the people are like?"

"What a strange question. But tell me about where you come from first. What are the people like there?" She asked.

"Oh my. It is a horrible place, cold and dirty. The sun rarely shines, and the people, well, they are not good. They are mean-spirited and cruel, they lie and cheat, and they are generally bad-tempered and not in the least bit friendly."

"Well." Said the woman. "That is what you will find up in the village, and those are the same sort of people you will meet there."

The man was very disappointed. He grumbled something that the woman could not understand but took to be a "thank you", turned around and walked back down the road from whence he had come. The woman continued her weeding.

A little while later, a second man appeared at the garden fence, and he too called her over. Once again, with her willow basket on her elbow, she went to see what he wanted. His shoes were as dusty and worn as the first man's had been.

"I wonder if you could tell me something?"

"Perhaps, perhaps not."

"That village up ahead. I must stay there for the night as the day is ending and my legs are weary. Could you please tell me how it is there? What are the people like?"

"That is the second time I have heard this question. First, you must tell me what it is like where in your village. How are the people there?"

"Oh, I come from a beautiful place, full of happiness and joy. The sun shines almost every day! The people are pleasant, friendly and kind. They look after each other, and everyone wears a smile."

"How extraordinary." Said the woman. "Because that is exactly how you will find the village when you get there."

With a graceful smile and a heartfelt "thank you" the traveller turned his eyes toward the village. He spent there a pleasant evening and a restful nights sleep.

Schönfelde, 03.03.2020

3

THE SELLER OF WORDS

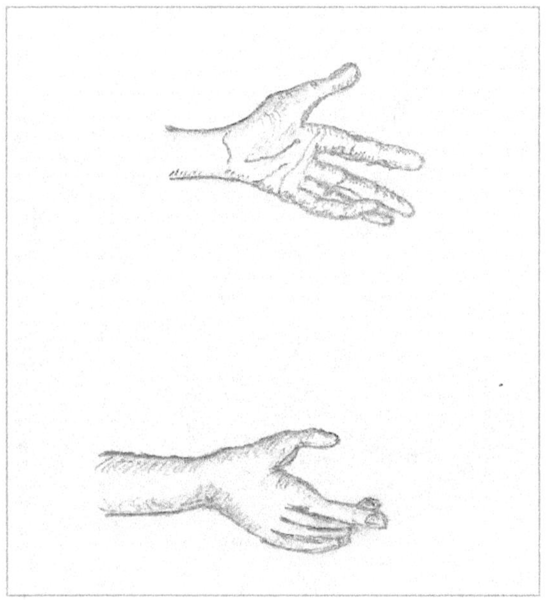

The character of a wise man who fools a sultan or a prince by selling him words can often found in Persian tales. The words the prince receives then become the thread of the tale. The word seller is, therefore, merely a facilitator to the story and, after doing his bit, is no longer of any importance. Such a character cropped up in a story I used to tell long ago, and it caused me to think. I wondered about him and thought how a story might be if he was at the heart of it. One day, while wandering through the back alleyways of Meknes in Morrocco, I saw, through an open doorway, a man, sitting on the floor of an otherwise empty shop. He was completely unaware of the world outside his door, and there did not seem to be anything ritualistic about the way he was sitting. His neighbours told me that he did that all day. I did not want to know anything about him, so I left it at that. He became the Seller of Words of this story.

Many centuries ago, in a city somewhere in the middle of a hot, dry and mountainous land, there lived a small man with a long grey beard who sold words.

He had a small shop deep inside the busy souk. A single dull oil lamp lit it, and he would sit on cushions, quite still, in the middle of the floor waiting for people to come.

And come they did. To buy words, of comfort or advice.

The small man with the long grey beard would have them sit on the floor before him, and he would listen to their motives for coming. The reasons were always different. Yet, at the core, all the same. They had either fears or fantasies, desires and passions, needs and wants, all very human and individual yet familiar to all.

So he listened.

Because to be able to sell words, you must first collect them. To do that you must learn to listen to them. Listen with all your being.

First, listen and then speak.

He was a good listener, which is why people came to him.

Afterwards, when they had said all they had needed to say, they would wait for the word sellers words.

When he spoke, he spoke softly and slowly, carefully choosing his words according to what he had learnt. Not so much from what they had said but more from how they had said it. Or perhaps what they had not said. For often in airing our questions, we declare the answers without recognising them ourselves.

He would never give a direct answer. He always found a story to tell. One that the listener could take away with them to ponder on. Within the tale, there would be many things for them to understand. Or not. That would depend on themselves.

Before leaving him, each of them would place a coin, perhaps two, in his bowl, and then they would return to from wherever it was that they had come. They would leave his little shop with his words in their minds, having left theirs with him.

These people were always relieved, happy, even elated when they left him, cured by the greybeards words. At least that is what they assumed.

For the truth was, and they were unaware of this, that it was not the little man's words that had enabled this marvellous transformation but their own. By merely speaking out, through expressing their fears and desires and giving those words a place in the world, they freed themselves of the weight of their worries. Their doubts were dispelled through their dialogue with the man. The change this brought upon them came not from the man but from within themselves. They had empowered themselves.

The small man with a long grey beard had quietly listened in reflection and let them do the talking.

Everybody has a story to tell. And the most considerable pain, so it is said, comes from having a story that one cannot tell.

Schönfelde, 09.02.2017

4

WHERE A SEED FALLS

This story has travelled far, as there are various versions of it to be found throughout collections of tales from Islamic countries. One can imagine it shortening a journey taken along a silk route long ago. Some are long and complicated, while others are quite concise. All of them confer wisdom upon the Kadi as he shows a willingness to listen to his pupils.

The story not only reveals a profound knowledge of the relationship between man and nature but also acknowledges the fundamental importance of youth and growth.

It is one of my favourite stories which I once had the pleasure of telling atop a roof garden in Marrakesh as the sun went down behind me and the Adhan, the call to prayer, sounded across the city.

It was early spring in a distant land where the winds which passed over the fields either blew down from the mountain or came from across the sea.

In this place, in a small village at the foot of the mountain, there lived two old friends. One had a small house and grew vegetables in his field. His name was Hakim. The other, Nadeem, lived in an equally modest house nearby where he kept a flock of goats which, each day, he took to graze up on the mountain.

Both men, to those who knew no better, might be considered pitiable but having all of the things that they required in life neither of them thought themselves to be so. Each was content with his lot, and neither sought more.

One afternoon, while Nadeem slept beneath a tree, thieves came and stole his goats. He was distraught. Left without a way of earning a living he shut himself up in his house and remained behind his door for days cursing his fate.

When Hakim realized that he had not seen his friend for some time, he went to the house where he found him in despair and thus learned of his friend's misfortune.

"What shall I do?" Asked Nadeem." How may I live now? I have no goats to milk. No meat to sell. No chance to earn my living."

Hakim thought for a while.

"My friend. We have been friends for many years. I cannot see you suffer like this so I will give you a half of my field on which you may grow some crops to sell. When you have earned enough money, then you can buy some more goats."

Nadeem protested.

"No, no. You will lose half of your income, and already you work all of the hours of the day to earn what you do, which is only ever just enough. How can you afford to let me have half of your field?"

"We are friends, and that is more important than anything in the world. It will help you."

"It will take so long for me to earn enough to buy new animals. When will I ever be able to repay you?"

"It does not matter. You are my friend, and that is what matters."

So what was said was done. Hakim marked out his field and divided it into two halves.

The mountain snow melted. The winds turned warm, and the birds sang from dawn to dusk. The two friends set to digging their halves of the field and began to think about the seeds they would plant. Nadeem, wishing to repay his friend's faith and generosity, worked longer and harder so he would reap a greater harvest. He would be the first of the two to bend his back to the earth, and he was always the last to clean his hoe.

One day Nadeem thrust the hoe into the earth and hit something solid. Curious, he dug deeper and saw that it was not a rock which he first expected it to be, but an old metal box. When he opened it, he found it to be full of coins. Gold coins.

He heaved the box up onto his shoulder and took it to his friend's house. He gave it to Hakim.

"You see," Nadeem said. "Fate is kind to you."

"What makes you say this, my friend?"

"Because fate planted a chest of gold in your field. You are rich and no longer will you have to work."

"But, Nadeem, the chest belongs not to me but you. I did not find it; you did."

"It is your field, Hakim."

"It was your hoe that found it, your hand that raised it and your shoulder that carried it here. It belongs to you."

"I cannot take any part of this gold after all you did for me."

"I cannot keep it either because I did nothing to earn it."

Unable to decide what to do with the gold, they went to see the Kadi who would know what the right thing to do would be.

The Kadi was sitting on his cushions, giving a lesson to three students who were training to become lawyers. When he heard what the two friends had to say he lightly pulled on his beard for a while, then turned to the young men.

"Here is an unusual case. You are scholars in law, and this would be a good time to show what this learning has made of you."

The first scholar wasted no time in answering.

"The land belongs not to one man nor the other but the Sultan. Therefore the chest and its contents belong to him."

The Kadi continued pulling at his beard as he turned to the second student.

"This is not so, my friend. Indeed the land does not belong to the two who stand here; it also does not belong to the Sultan. It belongs to the one who rules over us all. Allah. So, therefore, the gold should be given to the Imam. He must have it."

The Kadi tugged a little harder on his beard. The third scholar was quiet.

"And what do you say?"

"Well, I disagree with both of my colleagues. I feel that the issue here is not the prize but the reason for their hesitation. Neither of them is willing to see the other worse off than himself. That is a powerful friendship. Therefore I feel that their friendship deserves the reward, and the treasure must be used to celebrate this."

The Kadi had stopped pulling at his beard.

"How do you imagine that this might be done?"

"I would suggest that the gold be used to honour friendship in a way that everyone can appreciate its value; not just the Sultan or the Imam, but all. The gold should be put into the creation of a garden. A garden of friendship."

The Kadi expressed his pleasure in this idea and asked Hakim and Nadeem if they agreed. They did. Thus it was that the Kadi gave the gold to the young scholar and entrusted to him the task of travelling to the city and acquire the seeds to sow in the garden. The next day, with the blessings of the two friends, he set off.

The road was dusty, and the journey long. Along the way, he came to a Caravanserai where the young man found himself obliged to spend the night.

The following day he observed a large caravan of camels and mules preparing for departure. On the back of each beast, he saw cages. In the cages, he saw birds. There were many. They displayed such beautiful colours that it took his breath away. He inquired about them, and the merchant who owned them told him that he was bound for the Sultan's palace. When the young man asked what their fate would be, the merchant said that they were bound for the great golden cages in the Sultans' garden. The young man was overwhelmed with pity for the birds.

"If I was to offer you more than the Sultan would pay for them, would you sell them to me."?

"I am a merchant, so of course I would. But young man, where would you find such an amount. The Sultan is very rich."

The scholar produced the chest. The merchant saw that it contained far more gold than the Sultan had offered him and the deal was made. The merchant turned his caravan in the direction that the young man indicated, and they left the Caravanserai.

After a while, on the road, the young man stopped the procession. Then, to the astonishment of the merchant, he ran along the line of camels and donkey's opening the cages as he went. The birds flew up into the clear blue sky and away.

He was elated. He could imagine what the two men would say at his compassion. They would surely approve of such an act of kindness.

Or would they? And what would the Kadi say?

No longer able to go to the city to buy seeds he turned his eyes to the road back to home.

Each step that brought him closer to the village took him deeper into doubt. He had been responsible for a small fortune and asked to carry out a specific task. But that fortune was gone, and he had not carried out the job. Furthermore, he had broken the trust of the Kadi and the two friends. Realizing this caused him to dread having to stand before them to explain his actions.

Just before coming to the village, he sat down at the foot of a tree to consider his situation. The longer he did this, the worse he felt. He curled up on the ground and, with fearful thoughts, fell asleep.

He did not sleep for long; he was roused by a soft and sweet sound in his ear.

He saw the most beautiful of birds standing on his shoulder. In its beak, it bore a seed. He was captivated by the presence of such beauty and dared not move. The bird was so close to him that he could feel its heartbeat.

When the bird flew away from him, and he sat up, he saw that he was surrounded by birds. They were the birds that he had freed. And many more besides. Each one of them carried a seed in its beak. The young man rose and watched in awe as they took to the sky and flew toward the village where the two friends lived. To gather in the field where they lay the seeds into the earth.

Those seeds would, in time, become the flowers and the plants, the trees and the fruit of the garden that would grow and become known as the Garden Of Friendship.

"Where a seed falls, it will grow."

Essaouira, 22.01.2020.

5

A MORSEL OF KINDNESS

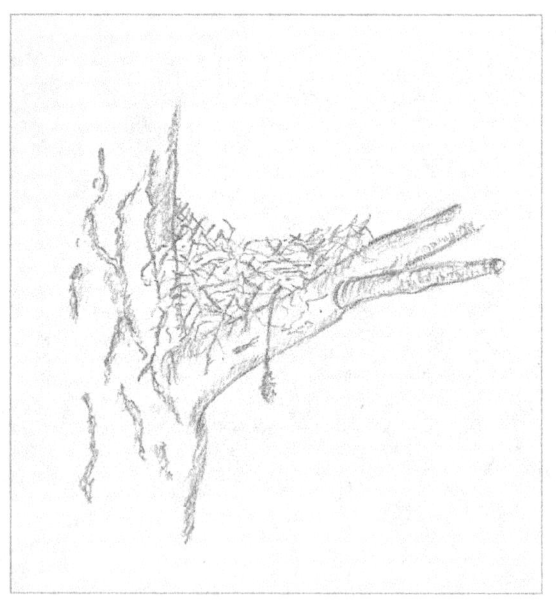

A poet, who lived in a village, went walking in the mountains to seek inspiration for a poem. Absorbed in his thoughts, he wandered high up to where the clouds lived, and there he got lost. When the rain came and threatened to soak him, he took shelter in a cave where a lioness had also taken herself away from the downpour. The poet saw her, and she saw him. Frightened for his life, he ran out of the dry cave and took to his heels. But the lioness was in no mood to get wet and, as she had recently eaten, she let the poet go.

Unaware of the lack of interest the lioness showed in him, the poet kept on running until he slipped and went tumbling down the steep slope of the mountain coming to a stop only when he crashed into a tree. When he came to, he found that he was trapped, by the leg, in the crook of two branches. No matter how he tried, he could not free himself.

The rain stopped and the night set in. It was cold, and by the morning he had a fever which left him delirious and weak.

So, unable to move or find food and, since no one knew where he was, it began to seem as if he might die there trapped in the tree.

As the days went by he grew weaker and weaker. He was afraid that each night would be his last but then one morning he saw that a pair of birds had started to build a nest just within reach of his outstretched hand. They seemed entirely unconcerned at his presence; indeed, it seemed to him that perhaps they regarded him as protection from predators. He watched as the nest grew, and soon there was a clutch of eggs within it.

The poet was becoming weaker, but the growth he observed in the nest gave him some sense of purpose. He was determined to see the eggs hatch.

Which, one day, they did.

Now he watched as the parents brought food to them in the form of worms and bugs. But one day one of them brought a morsel of bread which the bird left on the edge of the nest, just within reach of the trapped poet. He gratefully took it and put it into his mouth, feeling its goodness.

Every time the birds went searching for food for their chicks, they returned with pieces of bread. And each time they left one of them on the rim of the nest for the poet. Slowly he gained back his strength, and one morning he managed to free his trapped leg from the branches of the tree.

The last thing he saw before climbing down was the first of the fledgelings stretching its wings in the nest.

When he returned to the village, it was to greetings of joy, but when he recounted his story, he got only disbelief and mockery.

One morning, a few days later, the poet saw a bird flying above him heading out of the village. It was carrying a morsel of bread. He recognised it to be one of the birds that had saved his life. He watched patiently for the bird's return, and when it did, he followed it as it flew to a house nearby. There he saw it take some bread from a small heap on the window ledge. When he knocked on the door of the house, it was opened by an older woman. It was evident that she was quite poor. She invited the poet in and offered to give him some tea. He accepted the offer, and together they sat and drank.

"Do you put bread on the window ledge every day?" He asked.

"Oh, yes, every day."

"But you seem very poor. Why do you feed the birds when you can hardly feed yourself?"

"I love to see those birds come here. They are my only visitors. Besides, everybody, even the birds, needs a bit of kindness and kindness costs nothing." She said.

The poet looked at her with great admiration. "You have no idea what your kindness has done."

"I do not need to know. That is not why I am kind."

The poet never told her his story, but he did visit her every day. Sometimes he took her a bowl of hot soup, other times a sweet cake. Often when he sat with her, they would be still. Neither of them felt the need to talk.

38

Schönfelde, 10.03.2020

6

THE PATH OF TRUTH

I have enjoyed telling this particular story many times. If you ask any of the children in the schools where I regularly tell stories, they will tell you that I often begin by telling them that "this is one of my favourites". In this case, it is true. I especially love tales that involve a journey, a voyage of discovery.

Again, it is hard to know where this tale originates because there are so many different elements from various cultures and philosophies within it. Recently, I read a version set in North Africa where religious tones had clearly been embedded within it. However, by removing them, it was possible to detect a more profound sense of the fragility of human existence.

I found myself telling this story often while working in Kenya, and with each telling, it would adopt more of the landscape of East Africa and less than that of the North. It has, in my mind, remained there. Perhaps that is what happens to all stories.

A very long time ago in a beautiful lush valley, there lived two farmers. One of them cultivated a field at the top while the other tended his field lower down. Both worked all the hours that the gods allowed them in sowing, nursing and reaping the crops which they then sold on the market in the town nearby.

The field higher up the valley was productive as it was exposed to the sun longer than the one further down. When the rains came, they drained through the earth, irrigating the crops without saturating them. However, the same could not be said for the field below. The warming rays of the sun came to it late in the morning and left it early in the afternoon, which meant that no sooner had the earth warmed than it began to cool again. In this field, the crops were pale and thin.

So too was the man who worked there. His was a hard lot which was made more difficult by the meagre harvests. He struggled to eke anything out of the earth, which would earn him any money. Matters were made more critical, then when the rains fell. The shallow river in the valley would often over-flow, his field would flood, and the plants get damaged. The poor man was then left to start his work anew. Which, with a shrug of his shoulders and stoic resolve, he always did.

The man who farmed at the top of the valley had no such difficulties. Indeed, whenever the downpours destroyed the other man's crops, he was fortunate for he was then able to ask a higher price at the market for his produce due to there being no competition.

Therefore, over the years, one man had grown wealthy and the other poor.

One day, following a night of unusually heavy rainfall, the poor farmer went to his field to discover that everything had been washed away. Nothing at all had survived that he might be able to sell. He was ruined. His hard labour had been for nothing. How would he support himself? How would he pay for the seeds for his next crop? He denounced the fates that had sent the rain. Then he cursed the fate that had given him those fields in which to work. He sat on a rock at the edge of the sodden field and questioned the fairness of the world.

"I am harnessed to the yoke of my lot, shackled to a destiny I did not choose. Every day I bend my back to this earth, yet, at night I am hungry. Even the lowest creatures receive larger portions than I."

With nothing to trade or eat, he had no other choice than to go and ask his neighbour for help. But when he did so, he found little compassion. The rich man simply told him that being as it was not his fault that the man now found himself in such a situation, neither was it his responsibility to help him out of it. Indeed, if the man were fated to prosper, as he had, then surely the gods, in their eternal wisdom, would have granted him a more suitable field to tend. The unfortunate man went away and considered what he had heard.

Some days later, he returned to the rich man with a proposition.

"I do not ask for a handout, for that would offend you and humiliate me. Rather, I ask you, who I know to be a man of sound judgement, to consider ending the unfairness of my circumstances. I have warranted my fate no more than you have yours. It is within your power to turn a cycle of injustice into one of equity."

· · ·

"Explain how this might be done."

"Your field provides you with all that you need to live your happy and perfect life. I strive, bending my back to the ground, to grub a living from mine. But I get little in return, while you receive more than you need. Your field spared of damage from the rain is well-nourished. It receives blessings from the sun, whereas mine fated to be destroyed by one is ignored by the other. If you were to exchange the lower part of your field for the higher one of mine, then I would be freed from the weight of the misfortunes which presently burden me. I would be able to rejoice instead of lamenting the miseries I currently endure. You would lose very little if anything at all, whereas I would gain much. Such a gesture is in your power."

"But if I were to do that would I not be opposing the will of the gods? For it is they who set you in this predicament. Your part in the equation is to be as you are and nothing more or less. The cycle in which you dwell, the wheel upon which fate had placed you, turns as it must. It was decided so as you well know."

"Would the gods not wish for one to show to another a fair hand and help him in times of need?"

"This may be so. Nevertheless, I am unable to hand any portion of land over to you for its ownership is in the name of my son, who is still at his mother's breast. You would have to wait quite a time before you would be able to ask him. Besides,

I do not earn as much from the field as you seem to think. There are taxes to pay, and seed is expensive. I have labourers whose families I am bound to feed and clothe."

The poor man listened to a catalogue of reasons as to why the other could not help him, no matter how much he would have liked to do so. When the unfortunate man left, he no longer felt a sense of sadness at the injustice of the world; instead, he felt anger at the cruel lies of his neighbour. He was well aware that the son at the mother's breast was the youngest of others.

Later that evening, as he sat again on the rock by his field, he reflected on the sense of Truth. With just one sentence, which had been so obviously untrue, the rich man had managed to create an irrefutable case for not helping the other. False words, it to seemed the poor farmer, had much sway. But should it not be that true ones must have a higher worth?

The following morning he resolved to set out to seek for Truth, and if he were to find it, he would ask if this was not so.

His journey took him along a pathway which threaded its way between mountains, followed valleys and passed through villages and towns. Sometimes along the way, he saw others who, like him, lived their days bowing down in fields with their shoulders hunched to the pulling of hoes through the earth. Closer to the villages, he saw people carrying basketfuls of rice or vegetables to the market. Some had beasts carrying the burdens while others bore them on their backs or balanced upon their heads. Often he would walk beside them and engage in conversations into which he always slipped the same question; did they know where to find Truth? But the people laughed at him, telling him to leave them to get on with their business and for him to mind his own.

On he walked seeking Truth.

One morning, after leaving a small town, he took to a lonely path which stretched up to and over the horizon. Along the way, he saw a ploughed field and a man in it planting seeds.

"Greetings to you, my friend, could you tell me if this path will lead me to Truth?"

"It will if you consider death to be Truth." Replied the man without looking up.

"How so? What is your meaning?"

"Well, this path leads to a dwelling in which a wicked man lives. It is said that those who pass this place never return. So it must be that they meet their death, and so may you."

"Perhaps I will but perhaps not."

. . .

The traveller continued on his way. The man had not taken his eyes from his task.

The dwelling was a tumbledown hovel which had a roof of dried grass and thin, fragile walls. A man was chopping wood. When he saw the traveller approaching, he stopped his work and asked him what he wanted.

"I am seeking Truth, and fate has led me to follow this path. Please do not let me disturb you."

"You do not disturb me. I was about to stop. Come here and let me see you."

The traveller drew closer, enough to see that the axe was sharp and the hand that held it raised. But he was not afraid.

"Truth, you say? You are looking for Truth?"

"Yes."

"You are far from your home and impoverished, for I can see that your cloak is dusty and your shoes are worn. Why might that be, I wonder? And why is it that you seek Truth?"

"Because I am weary of listening to lies. False words have influence when they arise in the mouths of people who wield power, but true words of those who do not are rarely heard. I am tired of not hearing Truth or even seeing proof of its existence. My heart wishes to understand why this is so, and my head desires a fair share for myself in a just world. That is not a lot to ask for, I think."

"Indeed, it is not. Sit with me. Tell me about your journey." The man laid down the axe.

As they talked, it became clear to him that while his host could, without doubt, be a dangerous man, he was not about to do him any harm. He spoke well with carefully chosen words. The traveller saw that he kept an allotment well stocked with vegetables.

"I have not eaten a decent meal for some time. Would you allow me to prepare, on your fire, some of your vegetables for us both? That way, I can repay your hospitality as well as fill my stomach."

He cooked, and they ate. When they had finished, the man went into the house and returned with a small cloth bag.

"I will help you to continue on your journey, for it seems to me that your task is a good one, and your heart is right. Throughout my life, I have done some bad things, and this is why people call me a wicked man. I have stolen and cheated, but only to survive. I did not know what else to do. I let anger dictate my thinking, and by not listening to my heart, I have harmed others. I let the thirst for revenge govern my head. I accepted this fate. But you seem to be bent on changing yours. I want you to do something for me in return for this."

He held up the cloth bag.

"There are raisins in this bag, one for each bad thing I have done. They will help you and bring you closer to Truth. It is all I can give you. In exchange, when you find Truth, ask what is to become of me."

The path led the traveller over the horizon and, some days later, to a town. He came to a small shrine with painted white walls and light blue and gold trimmings around the doorway and its single small window. At the top of the steps leading to the entrance of the sanctuary, he saw a man rocking back and forth on his knees. He was quietly chanting. The traveller stopped at a respectable distance and waited for the man to finish his prayer.

"May I sit a while with you?"

"You may."

The man stood up, went into the shrine and returned with tea. The traveller offered his bag of raisins, which, once accepted, was quickly emptied.

. . .

The man explained that he was the keeper of the shrine, whose task was to pray for the people of the town who came and paid him to do so. He was overworked and tired. He said that the longer the prayer was, the more money he would receive, money which he used for the upkeep of the shrine. The rest he was hiding away for his old age. Thus, over the years he had amassed quite a small fortune so that soon he would be able to leave the shrine to somebody else. Inside he showed his guest a statue of an androgynous figure. It was slightly smaller than himself and covered with garlands and jewels. By day it was covered over by a silk cloth, and at night the doors of the shrine were shut. Only once, at midday, was it left uncovered and then only for a short while so that a few select people could, for a small fee, come and see it. He said that as he had never discovered the name of the god the figure represented, he had made one up. The visitors were satisfied with this. The name was just a word the devotees repeated while praying, he explained.

The following day as the traveller sat with the man as he prayed, a wealthy traveller arrived in a palanquin. The praying stopped, and he saw his host go to kiss the feet of the visitor who ordered a servant to lay two bowls of food out on the steps of the shrine. One dish was for the holy man and the other for the poor man. The traveller departed. The poor man noticed that while the bowl of the holy man contained a simple gruel, such as he received each day, his own had some chicken and fruit in it. The other saw this and swapped the bowls over saying that he was tired of the meagre fare they always gave him and he wanted something more sustaining instead. He disappeared into the shrine to eat the food so nobody should see him eat the meat which was supposed to be forbidden. From then on, each time a bowl of good food was given to him, it was taken away by the holy man, and he was left to eat the gruel. The shrine keeper told him to say nothing and said to him that he was welcome to stay for as long as he wished.

The man looking for Truth knew that it did not dwell in that shrine.

Before bidding his guest farewell, the keeper of the shrine made him promise to ask Truth what would become of him and to bring him the answer on his way back. He told him to be sure to mention all the supplications that he made for the benefit of others. The traveller said that he would.

His path now grew more arduous. The mountains became rugged and the terrain stonier and arid. The short days were hot and the long nights cold. He lost count of the days he had travelled. He simply continued along the way without question.

He began to weaken. Hunger gnawed at him, as did thirst. For seldom did it rain. But occasionally he found pockets of snow trapped between rocks, shaded from the sun. At times, as he walked, he became delirious. He began to think that he was hallucinating, seeing things. Bushes became sheep; clouds turned into trees and vice versa.

· · ·

Sometimes he had the feeling that he was not travelling alone. One afternoon, in his delirium, he imagined that someone was alongside him.

"What do you seek on this path, traveller?"

It was a man dressed in a modest kaftan which was of the most unusual shade of green, like the colour of woodland mist. Weather had tempered his face, and he had coal-black eyes and a long grey beard. On his head, he wore a turban of green. The same green that spring leaves have.

"I am seeking Truth." He simply replied.

"You have come far. I know, I have seen you many times. But you must know that while many seek Truth few men may see it. Fewer will recognise it when they do, and fewer still will understand what they have seen or heard. Your journey will be long, and it will only get harder."

The man turned to answer, but the greybeard was gone.

So it was that the road did become harder. Beneath his feet, the gravel became sharper and the soles of his shoes, worn thin, afforded no protection. One day he lost a shoe, but it was a while before he noticed it was gone. The path became less green and more grey. The cold cut deeper and closer to his bones. He slept on the side of the trail beneath thorn bush branches and with rocks for pillows. His skin became like the leather hides of the old oxen he used to see in the days before he became a lonely traveller in the wilderness that was the roof of the world. Whenever a snowstorm came, he put his head into it and with his shoulders hunched together managed to retain sufficient heat to prevent him from falling by the wayside and freezing to death. Then one morning, he awoke to see that the path led down out of the mountains and stretched across a vast desert plain. His journey was indeed long.

The plain was without life. The only thing that stirred was the sand, whipped up into his face by the wind. He had no idea how long he had walked, but he knew that the time of hallucinations and delirium were behind him, his senses were keener than they had ever been. Hunger was no longer a problem, his body seemed to be able to survive on air alone, and even thirst did not weaken him. Every day he covered long stretches of the path. When he was tired, he slept.

He came to an oasis. Tall, green trees wavered in murmuring breeze which rippled the surface of a small lake. He threw himself into the water, which was cold and fresh. It invigorated him and made him laugh. He drank and then lay on his back, naked in the sun to dry.

Then he saw an animal.

It was a camel, so thin that it seemed to be a miracle that it could still stand. Its fur fell from its back and legs and in patches. Its single hump was nothing more than skin, like an empty old sack. It was looking for something to eat but seemed to be oblivious of the luscious grass around it. The camel looked at him, and he saw that its eyes were sunk deep into its skull and that they had very little light within them. He sat up and called to it, but the camel did not respond and slowly wandered away.

The traveller now felt ready to move on. Usually, he would think of carrying water with him, but he had nothing in which to put it and besides he felt that there was no need. He had got this far without needing to carry water.

The days got hotter and the nights less cold. The mountains were long behind him, and the path was descending to a lower altitude. But he had no idea where he was. The land seemed to be made only of sand and stone. It was extremely dry. His tongue became swollen, and he cursed the lack of water. The air was as if someone somewhere had opened an oven door. Indeed, as he walked, he began to see signs of fire. There were remains of burnt trees as far as he could see. Soon everywhere he looked, he saw only black and grey ash. The landscape made him feel as if he was at the end of the world.

He was forced to sit and rest more often than he had done before.

Once more, he saw a camel. This one was scratching around in the ashes and charred branches of the trees. The camel was quite unlike the one he had seen at the oasis. This one was strong and sturdy. Its muscles rippled as it moved. Its fur was thick and shone in the sun. As the other had this one looked up at the man, and he could see that its eyes were full, bright and gleaming. The hump was almost gorged full. There cannot have been anything in that place left to eat, but the camel was chewing quite happily. Then it turned and walked calmly away.

The man felt no inclination to stay in such a desolate place.

Some days later, the path brought him to the end of the desert plains, and he found himself looking down into a fertile green valley. He found fruit growing on the trees, and there were nuts to eat.

The river that ran through the valley was a peaceful one. It was not wide, and its waters did not rush. Now, for the first time, he saw no clear path before him, and given the choice of walking upstream or down he had chosen up. The coolness of the flowing water and the softness of the grass made the walking pleasant. But by now, he was capable of walking any terrain. His strength was like that of an Ox and his stride that of the Leopard.

When he came to a bend in the river on the far side of it, he saw a beautiful white flowering tree. Below this tree, he saw a cave. Sitting in front of the cave was a man. He wore a kaftan the colour of the wooded mist which swirled about him and a turban the hue of the young leaves of the tree. The man gestured for the traveller to join him, pointing at a dip in the bank where some stepping-stones provided a means to cross the waters.

"So you are here. I anticipated that you would come. Welcome. Sit and drink."

From inside the cave, a blind, deaf and mute young man appeared bearing a tray of tea which he gently poured without spilling a single drop.

"You have questions."

"You know that I do."

"That is true. But you must know that here you might get answers to which you may not be able to reckon. Or even, perhaps, understand. We shall see."

The two men sat in silence. The night was falling, yet the older man did not offer the other a place to sleep, and neither did he seek one himself. He sat motionless. So his guest did the same. All through the night, they spoke without opening their mouths. Their thoughts enmeshed and became a single thought which travelled one path. The night was neither long nor short. It was night, and then it was not.

"Truth will come, then you may ask your questions. But when he does, you must not look at him. Not under any circum-stances. Your eyes must remain closed."

"How will I know when Truth is here if I cannot see him? How will I know when to speak my questions?"

"You will know."

The two men remained still, and the silence grew more profound. Time was longer of consequence.

"Truth is coming. Remember, keep your eyes closed."

A potter may form clay into a vessel, but it is the clay that will turn him into a potter. The traveller who, with a singular purpose, walks across the roof of the world, will learn much about self. It was now with the inner voice with which he spoke. His purpose had resolved into this moment. Aware of a compelling presence around him, he knew that he was in the presence of Truth. But how could he be certain? How could he see something without seeing it?

He opened his eyes at precisely the moment that Truth stood before him. The brightness, its strength was so intense that it almost blinded him. The pain of the light of Truth that burned into his eyes knocked him backwards, and he fell into unconsciousness.

When he came around, he was lying in the cave being tended to by the young blind, deaf and mute man.

"I warned you." Said the man.

"Am I blind?"

"You are not blind, you will regain your sight, but it will take some time. That time you will spend here in this cave away from the daylight, which might make things worse. You are fortunate that you are strong. Your journey here has put that strength into you. It has given you power."

So the traveller lived with the Dervish for some months. Each day, at dusk or dawn, for a few minutes, he went outside. Sometimes he sat by the river and listened to its voice. He drank its waters and felt stronger. He ate fruit from the tree, and gradually his sight was returned to him. One day he was ready to begin his journey back. The two men had spoken of many things, but there remained unanswered questions.

"So, my friend, it is time for answers. But first, you must ask the questions. Only the right questions will receive the answers."

"I met on my journey a man who was considered a bad man, he even admitted so himself. Before I left him, he made me promise to ask Truth what would become of him. Then I met a second man, a holy man who kept a shrine to a god; he too asked me to enquire of his future. But obviously, I did not get to ask either of these questions."

"I can give you your answers. I know Truth.".

"I know this. Please tell me."

"The man who is known as a bad man will have a calm and prosperous life. He will find peace and be free of rage. Indeed, he is finding it now because already he has taken the necessary actions to amend his past behaviour. By accepting his failures and mistakes, he will repeat them no more. Each raisin he gave you represented a mistake or a wrong deed, and by accepting his gift, you have helped him to leave the past. He is now free of the endless cycle of guilt and blame."

The two men now came to the edge of the river.

"The second man, the one who calls himself a holy man, will never live in peace. His life is built upon a falsehood. The riches he has stashed away have become the shrine. A shrine to his lying and dishonesty which sooner or later will crash down around him as dust falls from a shaking animal. A house built upon such fraudulence can only crumble. This man will spend the rest of his life sifting through the grime of his deception."

"I understand. You have answered my questions clearly. But I am puzzled as to the meaning of the camels which I saw."

The Dervish led the traveller to the stepping stones.

"One of them is you and the other your neighbour. For, you, like the camel in the ashes, thrived in the desert. But he, with his riches and comforts, will, as the camel at the oasis, become sick. One camel finds goodness despite the poverty around him while the other fails to appreciate the treasures that are below his feet. These two camels also show that, like the two men you encountered, goodness does not always reside where it seems to."

The man's hand was on the traveller's shoulder, guiding him to the stones which were the first steps of the path that would bring him home.

The return journey, as all return journeys are, was quicker. The man who had found Truth followed the same path back to his home that he had taken from it. It took him past two camels. One still finding sustenance despite being in the most inhospitable of places while the other continued to seem to be at death's threshold. When he came to the shrine, intending to bring the answer to its keeper, he found that he did not need to do so because the holy man, sitting begging on the filthy street, had already received his answer. So it was with the other man. He had transformed his house into a Caravanserai which prospered. He was now a wealthy and happy man. The traveller stayed there for a night, but his host did not recognise him. Such was his own transformation. For this reason, he did not give the man his answer either. There was no need.

When he finally came back to the valley where he lived, he saw that someone had dug his field and was busy planting saplings. It was a young man. He observed him for a while before going over to speak to him.

"What are you doing here?"

"I am planting trees. They will be perfect here where the soil is rich and strong."

"But it floods here quite often."

"I know this, but when they become established, the trees will grow tall enough to withstand the floods, and they will thrive. Look, I have dug the stream deeper so it will carry away the rainwater."

"Do you know whose field this is?"

"The farmer up the valley told me that it was his and I was welcome to use it. Any profits I make I am to share with him."

"Did he?"

On his way up the valley, the traveller saw that his neighbours' fields were, as usual, full of crops and his trees were flourishing. The house was close by so he went towards it, perhaps he might have a word with him. He found his neighbour sitting on the terrace. He was unshaven, and the end of his poorly wrapped turban hung loosely over his shoulder. His servant had brought him a tray with a pot of tea, but he had not noticed it. It had gone cold. When he approached him, the man did not seem to be aware of his presence. Staring vacantly over the valley, he appeared to be trying to say something, but the traveller could not understand what it was. He could see that the light in his eyes had grown dim.

The traveller left him then and went back down to the field that was no longer his. He turned up his sleeves and began to plant the tree saplings. He worked in silence beside the youthful man, who with great enthusiasm, told him of his desires and aspirations. When the first of the evening stars began to collect in the sky, the young man called him in for some food, and he went. He slept on the ground close to the open door, and the next morning he left.

He soon found the path again.

Essaouira, 27.01.2020

7

THE BLANKET

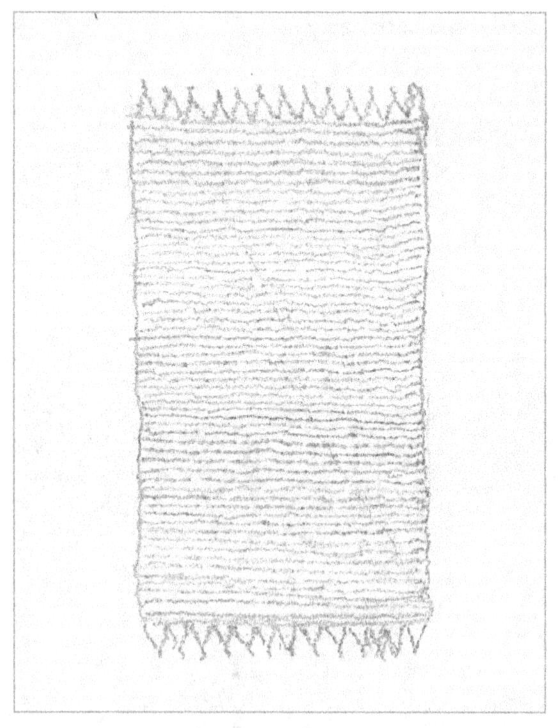

There was once a very rich merchant who wanted everything that he owned to be the best, the nicest and the most beautiful.

To make sure that he acquired the best, nicest and most beautiful things the merchant challenged the craftsmen who produced such objects to make them better than any other could. He did this by setting harsh conditions in which he also took a great delight. For example, the clockmaker was expected to ensure that the clocks he made neither gained nor lost time. The cooks were ordered to bake lemon cakes, his favourite, that were neither too sweet nor too sour and his gardeners were expected to grow different varieties of cherry trees in the orchard to be sure of there always being at least one in flower and that the trees were not to be allowed to grow too tall so that the merchant could enjoy their blossoms without having to strain his neck by looking upwards. And so on it went. Thus he ensured that the things that he had were always the best, the nicest and the most beautiful.

One day he decided that he needed a new blanket for his bed. For the one that he had was of the same colour and had the same pattern on it as others had on their beds. He wanted a blanket which was unique to him. The merchant called into his presence the most skilled and experienced of blanket weavers and gave them all the same task. He also gave them all the same challenge.

"Make me a blanket which is neither too long for my bed nor too short for my legs."

It was made clear to them that they were privileged to be given such an undertaking, but if the blankets did not meet the requirements of the merchant then they should not expect to be paid for their efforts.

Thus, the weavers, as soon as they sat themselves at their looms, all found the task set to them too great a challenge. Unsure how to make such a blanket, they had no idea where to begin. Each of them had measured the merchant's bed and his legs and each had calculated how long the blanket should be, but all of them suspected that there was a catch somewhere and that no matter what they produced it would not be right, and then they would have done the work in vain for they would not be paid. But the merchant would get to keep the blanket.

However, one wily weaver had an idea. An idea which would more than fulfil the task.

The wool he chose was the finest he could get. The colours were complimentary to one another and perfectly reflected the merchant's taste. The pattern he used was both stylish and unique. The blanket that stretched out across the loom was, in his eyes, almost perfect. But to make it really unique it needed just a final touch.

The weaver wove the dried stalks, leaves and flowers of some nettles in between the final threads of the weft and the warp of the blanket.

When he was presented with the blanket the merchant was most impressed and said so. He looked at the weaver with admiration. He ordered his servants to make up his bed with the new blanket.

"But, my dear man, if this blanket is too short or too long then I won't pay you anything for it."

The blanket fitted perfectly on the bed so it wasn't too long. The merchant then removed his shoes and socks and climbed into his bed. The weaver watched and waited. The merchant stretched his legs out as far as he could and, as he planned, his toes popped out at the bottom of the blanket. He smiled.

"The blanket is too short for my legs! You see, my feet are sticking out."

But then he began to feel a strange burning, stinging sensation on his ankles. The pain became too much to bear and he pulled his feet back up away from the nettles which were woven into the end of the blanket.

"But no." Said the weaver. "It seems to be of the perfect length for your legs. Look ,you cannot see your feet."

The merchant paid the weaver handsomely who left him with a smile and a wish.

"May you live in peace as the rest of us do… By stretching our legs according to the length of our blankets"

Schönfelde, 23.03.2020

8

THE MAN WHO SAT LIKE A ROCK

H ere we have a very simple Sufi tale.

Like all such tales, their purpose is to open the mind of the listener. Often they are referred to as "teaching tales", but I think that that does them and the listener an injustice. It avoids the point that teaching does not mean merely telling pupils something which they do not yet know but, more importantly, helping them to see things that they do know but are failing to recognise.

In a valley which caught the sun for just a short while each day there lived a man. He had made his home in a cave and his intention was to contemplate the meaning of things. To that end he would pull his knees up to his chest and sit without moving in front of the cave for hours on end. He was so still that from a distance he looked like a rock because the grey hue that everything wore in the valley had also seeped into his skin.

Each day, at a time written in the stars, the sun would pass overhead and the man would look up. He wondered what it must be like to be as the sun. To be able to view the world from up on high rather than, as he did, from the depths of a grey, dim valley. He could hardly imagine the beauty that the sun might witness on his travels. He thought about these things as he sat in front of his cave with his chin on his knees. Sitting as still as a rock.

One day, as he saw the shadows hide themselves from the coming light, he wondered again about what the sun might see and as soon as he himself was bathed in light he looked up and shouted out.

"Hey, Sun. What is it that you see on your travels?"

The Sun seemed to pause for a moment and then replied. "The beauty of the everything in all its glory and splendour".

The man watched the Sun move on, saw the shadows come out of hiding to reclaim the valley and pulled his knees back up to his chin.

And the words of the sun echoed in his ears….

Looking into his cave he saw how dark and cold it was. He saw only grey dampness and thought that the sun was very lucky not to live as he did.

Some days later the man who sat like a rock gathered up the courage to ask the Sun another question.

"Would it be possible to see that which you see?"

The Sun told him that if he believed it to be so he could, and the man found himself next to the Sun looking at the earth. It was true. The beauty, the splendour, the colours! How bright and shining it all was. In every direction he looked he saw something marvellous.

"And how do you find it all?" Asked the Sun.

"Truly beautiful." He replied. "You are so lucky to live in such a way. My home is dark and cold. It is grey where I am. There is no beauty."

And he invited the Sun to come and see.

The Sun followed the man down to the valley and to the cave.

Inside the man turned to the Sun.

"Do you see the difference? Nothing like you get to see everyday."

The Sun looked around and then turned to the man who sat like a rock and said.

"I do not see the difference."

Moulay Bouzarqtune, 14.01.20

9
SOUL CAGES

I n the middle of the Neues Kranzler Eck in Berlin, two
minutes walk from the Zoologischer Garten and the train
station that bears its name, there are two large bird pens. In
them, there are birds. Tropical, colourful and caged.

One morning in late May, I arrived in Berlin on an earlier
train than I usually did and far too early for work. To pass the
time, I decided to walk to school. It was a warm morning with
the promise of a lovely day. The walk took me past those
birdcages.

At that time of the day, it was just before seven, my brain is at
its most sponge-like. Early mornings are good for my mind. It
is open and aware, and, still uncluttered by the matter of existence, it sees things clearly.

I stood before the bird cages. The two pyramid-shaped enclosures, themselves confined in a square of tall glass and steel
buildings, were pointing mockingly to an open sky that the
birds within would never know.

An immediate rush of anger surged over me as I watched
them gliding round within the restrictions of the cage. At
reaching the mesh, the limits of their freedom, they would pull
up in sudden surprise, as if slamming on air brakes. One very
colourful bird repeated this over and again. Its instinct, inca-
pable of recognising the existence of constraint, was forced to
accept it. I was enraged.

As a young man, in my Laurie Lee[1] period, I had travelled through Spain and for a while, sick of and from picking chemically dusted mandarins for a living, I worked with a Italian circus. My job was to clean out and prepare the elephants for the evening show by tarting them up with spangled headbands and shiny toe-nails. In the beginning, I loved it. I presumed I was adventurous and romantic. Like the authors, I carried around in my rucksack Lee, Hemingway or Kerouac[2]. I was lean, windswept and smelled of elephants. But the fascination soon faded. Seeing, and worse, hearing those gentle beasts as they were prodded into the ring by handlers with electrified pokers was not pleasant. The naive dreamer that I was, ached to whisper into their ears. "Please go in there."

At the end of the performance, they were fettered and put out in enclosures to feed. At night still hobbled, they were chained to palettes, barely large enough on which to lie down. More often than not, they would spend the night standing up, and I vividly remember, watching them sway from side to side, lifting their feet as far as the chains would allow. I would squat by the bales of straw, fascinated. Then I realised what they were doing. They were marking time, walking on the spot. Going in the minds where they would have gone, had they have been able to roam freely. But they weren't free, and those chains let them go nowhere. Their eyes were sad and dull. Small wonder.

In Valencia, on Christmas Day, I left the circus and the elephants emptied of romantic ideas and filled with a dislike of chains. And those that apply them.

I recalled those elephants that morning in Berlin while watching the birds, confined to their small pocket of freedom. Surrounded by glass, concrete and metal, they were expected to behave naturally enough for us to delight in the joy of watching birds. I felt a complete and utter disgust toward those cages. And then toward myself. There I was watching them and I could and would walk away without lifting a finger to end this cruelty, instead of pulling out a knife and slashing the mesh. Twenty years earlier and I would have done just that. I always carried an Opinel in those days.

On the way up Kuhfürstendamm, I tried reasoning with myself. I was older and wiser and understood that by liberating the birds, I would be culpable for their deaths. They couldn't survive in the wild, especially not in a city. Moreover, trashing the cages would be vandalism. Blah, blah, blah. On and on, my thoughts went gradually releasing me from the responsibility of having to honour my values. And my feelings of disgust. It is how it is I told myself. But I knew well enough that through those arguments I was copping out.

Anyway, I was as much trapped in the system as the birds were... I had to go to work.

The Ku'damm is one of the busiest streets in Berlin. But not at seven in the morning. The big department stores don't open until ten o'clock. It was almost deserted, there were no shoppers, tourists or building workers. There were few cars and even fewer buses.

As I walked along, I looked around, back in sponge mode, absorbing all I saw. And without the distractions of other bodies or vehicles, there was much to see. Shops with their doors closed, without shoppers in them, are just buildings. Plenty of glass yet dark inside, like turned-off televisions whose screens reflect the room that they are in. Passing a well-known sportswear shop, I saw, on the other side of the glass, a cleaning woman with a vacuum cleaner. (Who calls them that these days?) She was middle-aged and had a worn-out look about her as if she had not been taken care of as a child. The doors were locked, and she was inside only a metre or two distant from me. But the glass separated us. I watched her for a while and thought to myself. "Here's another bird".

She was not happy in that shop which was full of bright, shiny things. It was not her natural habitat. That was obvious from her bearing. As she laboured, pushing the cleaner around, she rarely looked up, out through the glass to the outside world. I could not but help comparing her to the birds. "Smash the glass, let her out," I thought. Yeah, yeah. More misplaced idealism.

Walking on, enjoying the sunshine and the anticipation of work, I realised that instead of having to fight to destroy cages, we should strive against the construction of them. We should never ensnare anything in the first place. But that is easier said than done of course.

I was on my way to school and the world of storytelling.

As I turned into the road where the school was, I remembered something I had heard somewhere. It had been a story told to me quite hastily, almost 'by-the-way'. But the essence of it stayed with me. It was from Rumi.

As I walked along, I let the story weave itself in through my mind. By the time I sat down in the classroom, and the children had settled down to listen, the story was ready to be told.

There was once a merchant who came from the south to settle in the north of the country. He was good at being a merchant and had become prosperous. With his profits, he had built a large elegant house. The merchant was proud of his wealth and wished to flaunt it.

In the hallway, there was a pair of striking staircases, built in the shape of two flower petals, which led to the upper floors. The merchant had had a library built, the shelves of which he filled with expensive and rare books. The important books he exhibited at lower levels so that his guests would notice the titles and be impressed by his intelligence. In all of the rooms, there were fine tapestries and rugs. The dining-room tastefully decorated in bright colours which were not gaudy but lively. Here, a large mahogany table dominated the room. There was an abundance of silver candelabra. Paintings and rugs hung from the walls. The many bedrooms of the house were no less splendid, and his guests always marvelled at their airy character.

To keep the house in order, he employed a butler, a cook and some servants. He regularly invited people to dine with him to show off his wealth and his delicate taste.

On warm evenings, when he was alone, he would sit in the elegant garden, which had been created by the best designer in the land. Here he could enjoy the perfumes of the flowers on the fresh air while he drank the most expensive wines. It was all very magnificent.

But the garden was not complete. The merchant felt that it was missing something. He wondered long and hard about what that might be. Then one day, he decided that he needed a bird. A bird which would remind him of the sounds he had heard as a child when he had lived near to a forest full of birds. Yes, that was it. He needed a songbird.

He hired a trapper and paid him to travel to the forest in the south to catch such a bird.

The trapper returned with a beautiful songbird in a gilded cage, and the merchant was pleased. He hung the cage in a small pavilion in the garden. Whenever the merchant sat nearby, the bird sang and its song did indeed remind him of his youth.

When he invited them, his guests were amazed by the stair-case, the dining room and the garden. They were impressed by his library and the books. But above all, they were charmed by the songs of the bird in the golden cage. The merchant delighted in this. From then on, he needed no reason when inviting guests and they, in turn, found none not to accept.

One day the merchant decided to travel back to his birthplace to do some business. In a generous mood, he summoned the butler, the cook and his tailor to ask them if there was some gift that he could bring each of them from his journey. The butler requested a particular tunic, found only in the south, that would make him stand out more and therefore better reflect the merchant's taste. The merchant wrote this down in a pocketbook and turned to the cook. He asked for spices that were not be found in the north and which would make the food he put on the mahogany table unique, once again reflecting the merchant's taste. This, too, was written down in the little book. Next, he asked his tailor who said that he wanted a fine cloth which was woven only in the south so he could fashion a cloak for the merchant. The merchant wrote this down, smiling. The servants also asked for items that would improve their work and thus the merchant's pleasure. He was happy about this.

The evening before he was to travel, the merchant sat alone in his garden and meditated. When he had finished, he heard a voice behind him.

"What about me?"

The merchant looked around but could see no one.

"Yes, me. What about me?"

He saw that it was the bird that had spoken.

"What about you?"

"You have asked everybody what they want, but you have not asked me."

The merchant went up to the bird and asked him what he might want.

"I want you to open the cage for me. Let me out. Set me free. You will not be here to enjoy my song so let me out."

"When I return, I will wish to hear your song. Besides, you are the most wonderful thing in the garden. My guests would be so disappointed if you are no longer here. I'm sorry, but I cannot let you out."

"I thought you would say that. So, please, I want you to go into the forest near your home, for you and I come from the same place. Go to the hill in the middle of the forest where the trees are taller than all the rest and whose leaves are of a green incomparable with other leaves on any other tree in any other forest. I want you to shout out about me. Tell the birds there that I am locked in a cage and cannot return to them, for they are my brothers and sisters, my uncles and aunts, my family. Tell them, so they will know where I am and no longer be worried for me. Tell them that I live and, but for this cage, I would fly with them again in that forest."

"This I will do." Said the merchant.

He left the next day, riding his favourite horse. He was accompanied only by a few servants.

A week later, after a pleasant and peaceful journey, he arrived in the land of his birth. He went to his family home and got straight down to business.

After he had spent some time with his family, he went into the city and took out the pocketbook with the list of requests. One by one, as he bought them, he ticked the items off and soon he had all that was required. He prepared to travel back north, to his beloved home.

The journey up was as uneventful as the journey down had been. As the merchant rode along the edge of the forest, he was glad to hear the bird song that reminded him of his youth. It also reminded him of the bird's request. He ordered his servants to wait for him and walked into the forest. It didn't take him long to find the hill with the tall trees.

He walked to the top and began to shout out. To start with, he felt it an absurd thing to do, but it was what the bird wanted.

So he cried out even louder. The forest fell silent. As if every living creature within it was listening to him. He began to enjoy himself, finding it quite exhilarating. He cried out everything that the bird had asked him and then stopped and listened to the silence. He heard a rustling sound above him and looked up. On the tallest branch of the tallest tree, he saw a bird. As beautiful as the one in the cage in his garden.

It was quivering. Suddenly it leaned out from the branch at an odd angle and fell, twisting in the air as it did. It landed with a thump onto the forest floor below.

Realising that his words must have killed the bird, the merchant was shocked.

"Surely, it was the brother or sister of the bird in my garden. Perhaps even his mother. The news I gave has broken its heart, and it has fallen to its death."

Pale and saddened the merchant left the silent forest without looking back. He returned his journey home.

A week later he arrived, cheered to see his home again. The household was pleased that he had had a safe trip. The butler looked splendid in the new jacket. The cook was delighted to be able to prepare even more remarkable meals, and the tailor got straight down to work on the new cloak. How happy the merchant was.

But he avoided the garden. He was not looking forward to telling the bird about what had happened in the forest.

Some days later he had guests and after the dining and the drinking were over, they all went to sit in the garden. It was a pleasantly warm evening. The wine was smooth and the conversation light. The bird in its golden cage was singing. Eventually, his guests left, and the merchant found himself alone in the garden.

"Well?”

He tried to ignore the bird.

"Did you do as I asked?"

He went to the cage but couldn't look at the bird; instead, he stared down at the ground as he spoke. He was sad, but more than that, he was ashamed. But he told the bird, in every detail, precisely what had happened.

When he had said all that there was to say he looked up.

The bird was trembling. It leaned out from its perch at a strange angle and fell, with a thump, onto the cage floor. The bird lay lifeless on its back.

The merchant was so shocked that he didn't respond at first. He just stood there staring at the beautiful bird, feeling deep shame. Then he opened the cage door and reached in. Gently he picked up the bird's body and held it to his heart.

"I must have killed it with the news, just as my words had killed the bird in the forest. It is my fault. I have broken their hearts."

Tears began to fall from the merchant's eyes as he held the bird in the palms of his hands.

Then the bird stood up. It spread its wings and flew away.

His tears of sadness turned to tears of joy and laughter as he realised what had happened.

The merchant never put anything in a cage again.

………

I have told this tale many times since. In one class, during the discussion that inevitably takes place at the end of any story, a student said that he understood the story well because he saw classrooms as cages. He felt trapped within their walls.

"Well," I said to him, "that depends…. You could see this place where you can learn, as a key rather than a lock."

The question most asked in the discussions about this story is
if the bird in the forest died or not. I never answer the question because I do not have one to give.

Schönfelde, 05.03.2017

---

1. If I had not have read "As I walked Out One Midsummer Morning" then, I
   am sure, I would not have walked out one midsummers morning….
2. As much as Midsummer Morning moved me, literally, so did "The Road".
   Indeed one of my dearest travelling companions was, like the alias of
   Kerouac'sreal-life companion, named Dean. But Dharma Bums was the
   book I carried in my pocket in those days.

10

THE MERCHANT'S MEAL

A version of this story, there are a few, was collected by the British missionary to Kashmir, the excellent Rev. J Hinton Knowles in his Folk Tales From Kashmir which was first published in 1887. He titled the story the "The Man From Shiraz". In a footnote, he informs us that Shiraz is a city in Southern Persia. A tale then very much from the glorious days of the adventurous travel.

There was once a merchant who had become, over the years, very rich. He took a good deal of pride and pleasure in his wealth and whenever he had visitors, which was often, his table was always well laden and none would leave without having tasted the delights of the finest food available.

Now, one time a man came to the city where the merchant lived to do some business. He happened to be an old friend of the merchant and was keen to see how he was faring after having not seen him for such a long time. The man sent a note informing the merchant of his presence in the city and wondering if he might call the next day. The merchant read the note and duly replied with a third note which told of his joy at the thought of seeing his old friend and that he would be expected at seven o'clock the following evening. This note was replied to with a confirmation.

The merchant put his cooks to work to prepare a meal for his guest at the stated time. The visitor arrived and compliments were exchanged. The visitor presented his host with a small bottle of rose water which his wife had made and was also the product of his business. The merchant lead his guest to the table and bid him to sit. The cushions were comfortable and the table was lit by lamps and candles. The food began to arrive. A fish soup with herbs and lemon was presented to the diners. While the merchant's bowl was filled almost to the brim the visitor allowed just a small amount to be put into his and quietly he sipped his soup. The merchant talked of his achievements as the visitor listened.

The dishes that followed were innumerable and each more delicious than the last. The merchant greeted the arrival of each course with great delight and a comment that nowhere in the land would his friend find a more pleasurable sight than the one before him. He would then eat with relish. But the visitor would only take a small morsel from each of the dishes presented to him and indeed of some he took nothing at all. After a while the merchant noticed this and began to wonder as to why this was. Perhaps, he thought, his friend had eaten earlier in the day. No matter, he would enjoy the meal. And so he did.

"Was the sweetness of the orange curd and the small biscuits not quite exquisite?" The merchant asked as he threw his napkin onto the table indicating that he was satisfied.

"It was."

"But you ate so little."

"I have little appetite for such food."

"How strange! But the meal was to your liking?" Asked the merchant.

"It was, but you see, where I come from we do not eat in a such a way."

"Oh really? Then I am sure that it must be quite strange for you if you are not accustomed to such food."

"Indeed. The food in my house is far better than this."

The merchant was at a loss as to what to say. The visitor rose from the table and, giving thanks, made his way to the door. Their parting, while amicable, left the merchant with a strange feeling that something had gone wrong.

The next day, as he went about his business, the merchant felt cheated. He felt no joy in knowing that his friend was used to better food than he. The idea that his hospitality had not been good enough hurt his pride. He sent a note to his friend inviting him to dine with him again that evening, and once again the cooks were set to work. This time they would surpass the previous evening's efforts.

That evening, when the visitor arrived, he was welcomed and shown to a table which was already laden with delights. The colours and the smells were almost overwhelming. There were meats of many kinds and steamed vegetables arranged in heaps between platters of different breads and dried fruits. Mounds of couscous and rice steamed gently in their bowls. The visitor sat on the cushions and his host bade him to eat. Again the merchant piled in to the food and with great gusto filled his plates and his mouth with all that he saw before him. The visitor took little. Perhaps even less than he had done the previous evening. The merchant saw this and was perturbed.

Again, when the meal was over the merchant complimented the food and asked his guest what his opinion was. Again his friend said that the food in his house was better.

As soon as the door had closed behind the visitor, the merchant was almost in a rage. "How dare the man be so rude. How dare he be so ungrateful. How dare he!"

The next morning the merchant sent another note of invitation. Then he himself went to the market to buy the food for that evening's meal. He engaged two extra cooks and the kitchen became a hive of energy and industry.

The visitor arrived to see a table that was so laden with food it seemed that it could not bear the weight for much longer. He sat and the merchant began to explain what had been prepared.

"The birds that you can see come from the upper reaches of the rain forest and they breed only once every two years.

Their meat is so precious that only a handful of people ever get to see it, let alone taste it. The fruit that you see comes from a tree which grows only on an island far to the south of the country. It is so precious that only a handful of people can afford it."

The merchant went on taking pleasure in describing the food on the table. Then he began to eat. Rapturously he partook of each dish pausing only to look up and see how his guest was enjoying himself. But his guest was not enjoying himself. With less on his plate than the evenings before the man ate very little. Of the bird from the forest he ate nothing. The merchant, seeing this, lost his temper.

However he spoke cooly.

"My friend! Here at my table you sit and you treat the food the best cooks in the land have prepared for you with such disrespect and scorn! For my satisfaction I must ask you why this is."

"It is fine food. I have no doubt. But, as I have already told you, the food at my table is better."

The merchant again was speechless. The visitor left.

Some months later the merchant found himself in the town of his old friend. Remembering what had passed and keen to find out what was meant by the food at the other's table being better than his the merchant sent a note.

That evening, after reading the replying note, he knocked on the door of his friend's house. He was let in and shown to a low table surrounded by cushions. His friend, now his host, greeted him and went into the kitchen. He returned with three bowls. One with rice, the second with vegetables and the third with semolina sweetened with honey. He wished the merchant an enjoyable meal.

Thinking that his host had had no time to prepare any better food, the merchant ate what was before him and after he was satisfied, for the honey sweetened semolina had been rather good. He informed his friend that he would like to return the following evening and reminded him of the food that he had spoken of being better than that at his table. The host would be pleased to see him again and would prepare the best meal that he could.

The following evening the merchant arrived at the house of his friend and was shown to the table. On it were three bowls. The same as the evening before. The merchant was shocked. Then he felt cheated again. Then he felt insulted.

"My friend. You told me that the food at your table was better than at mine! But this is definitely not so. This food is worth nothing. How dare you be so rude to me."

"I disagree with you, my dear friend. You see, the food you put on your table is for only a few people to enjoy, there is nothing good about that. Also, by taking such rare birds for their meat you are ensuring that there will be no such birds in the future. The same applies to the fruit. Your choice of food is unsustainable. As is your style of living. My food however harms no animals. Nor does it harm nature in any way. In fact, to produce such food one must work in harmony with nature. The food on my table is sustainable and none of it will be wasted. This is why I say that the food on my table is better than yours."

The merchant was, once again, lost for words.

Essaouira, 10.02.20

THE GOLD BENEATH THE BUSH

This is a Chinese tale. In a similar way to Hakim ad Nadeem one may feel such sympathy for the pair in this story. It is a beautiful and simple tale to tell.

Once, many, many years ago, there lived two friends who had known each other since their days at school. These two men, like Damon and Pythias, loved each other and, when their work allowed, were always, in each other's company. No cross words passed between them and no unkind thoughts marred their friendship.

One was a book-keeper who spent his days, from early morning until long after the evening sun had set, in the offices of the local government filling in ledgers with numbers and calculations. His room was in the lowest part of the building where he hardly ever saw the sun.

The other man also worked in a government office. His job was writing down and recording the discussions had by the officials, which, of course, were long-winded and endless.

The two men were each allowed an afternoon of freedom once every fortnight and sometimes, but not often it was on the same afternoon.

It was a bright, beautiful day in early spring when they set out for a stroll together in the forest. The previous evening had been stormy, and now the trees were soaking up the rain. The air was clear and fresh, and the ground was soft beneath their feet.

They were tired of the city, its noises and its thick damp air. They wanted, just for a while, to breathe as well as think, freely.

"Let us find the heart of the forest," said one. "Surely there we can smell the sweetness of the flowers and lie on the moss-covered ground. Then we will forget the jobs that we are doing and the work we will have when we return."

"Yes," said the other, "the forest is an excellent place to be now."

With a slow and mindful pace, they passed along the winding road. The two men spoke little but instead let their eyes turn in longing toward the distant tree-tops. Their hearts beat as one as they walked deeper into the woods and their pleasure with the afternoon grew.

"For thirty days I have worked over one edict," sighed the one who was the clerk. For thirty days, I have not written any word other than one spoken by the awful windbags in the government. My head is stuffed so full of senseless verbiage, that I am afraid it will burst. How soothing the breath of the forest is. The sound of the pure air blowing through the trees is a delight compared to what I have to hear all day."

"I too have had little respite from my books. While you copy words, I must juggle numbers between columns and rows. They dance now before my eyes! My master is a stickler for detail and accepts no errors, and I must be so attentive that I think my mind will implode!"

They came to a clearing, and after crossing a little stream, took an almost forgotten path which led them between young green trees and wild shrubs. For an hour or so they rambled on, sometimes talking at other times silent, each with their own thoughts.

Upon hearing the beautiful song of a forest bird, they stopped next to a thicket of flower-covered bushes, to listen for a while. One of them saw, on the ground brightly shining from under the bush before them, a nugget of gold.

"You are rich!" Said the other.

"Why me?" Came the reply.

"Because you saw it first. It is yours."

"No, my friend, I think that you should have this treasure. Because your work has kept you and will keep you in your lightless office for longer than mine."

"But your work has you seeing the riches of others without giving you any for yourself. Surely you deserve this gold rather than I."

"I cannot, with a clear conscience, take this with knowledge of the hardships you will have to bear."

"That is the same as my reasoning for refusing to deny you of this wealth. You deserve this more than I."

Thus they discussed for some minutes, each refusing to take the treasure for himself; each insisting that the other was more deserving of it than they.

"Listen to us! We begin to sound like the politicians I have to work for every day."

"Or the speculators whose money I record in the thick books of my office."

"This is not the reason that we are friends."

"And gold is not the reason that we came into the forest."

"We will leave it where it is and continue our walk."

So, they left the chunk of gold in the very place where they had seen it, and the two friends walked away. Each happy because he valued his friend better than anything else in the world. Thus they turned their backs on any chance of quarrelling.

"It was not for gold that we left the city." Said one.

"No," replied his friend. "One day in this forest is worth more than any nugget."

"Let us find a comfortable spot to rest before we continue. The day is still young."

They found a green grassy knoll beside a spring that seemed to be just the right spot, but they were sorry to see it already occupied. A woodcutter was taking a break from his work. He had stretched himself out at full length on the ground and was settling down to take a nap.

But the presence of the two friends disturbed him. With a scowl, he sat up and shouted in their direction.

"So, two city dwellers come into the forest, and they can't keep themselves from disturbing a poor hardworking woodcutter. Be off with you and leave me in peace."

The friends looked at the man and noted how rough he looked. His clothes were shabby and torn. Each was thinking of the gold nugget.

"This man deserves the gold far more than you or I." Said one to his friend.

"I agree. Let us tell him of it".

They did so by explaining how they had come across it. That being friends they could not decide who should profit from it so rather than falling out over something that only one of them could have they had left it.

"Now we see that we made the right decision for we have met you and it is clear that you should be the one to take it. It will mean the end of your troubles."

The woodcutter was up and away down the path to where the friends had described the nugget to be.

"I'll be rich! No more swinging my axe. All thanks to two foolish city dwellers!"

Feeling pleased by what they had done but less so with the manner of the ungrateful woodcutter, the friends walked on. Soon the gold nugget was forgotten. The bird song grew louder, and the scents from the forest floor became sweeter.

At last, they came to realise that the time to turn back was near.

They shared the bread that one had brought and the other's fruit and then, reluctantly but in good humour, turned to retrace their steps.

At the grassy knoll by the stream, they saw the woodcutter. Who, upon seeing them, let out a shout so vitriolic that it took them aback.

"You liars have tricked me! How funny do you think it was to go running through the forest thinking that riches lie in wait only to be disappointed and indeed, almost killed. What depraved minds you two have to think up such a trick to play on a poor old woodsman. Shame on you!"

The two friends were perplexed with the man's behaviour for he was in such a rage that they could hardly placate him. When they did, he explained his fury.

"I found the place you described. Upon lifting the branches of the bush, I saw a glint of gold, just as you said I would. But on reaching in to get at it, I realised, just in time I might add, that it was a venomous snake. I was lucky not to have been bitten by the monster! You wanted to play a trick on me and have me killed! Luckily for me, I had my axe with me, and I could chop him with it. Otherwise, you would have been murderers!"

Finally, the friends calmed him down and tried to tell him that that had not been their intention, but the woodsman was not convinced. They left him before he got angry again.

They did indeed feel quite ashamed at the trouble they had caused. It had been an easy mistake to make for they knew nothing of the ways of the forest and little realised that snakes could lie under every bush.

They were interested to see one. So when they came to the bush, they crept up toward it with great curiosity and no less trepidation.

"Look, see it is gleaming under that low bough." Said one.

The other, using a short stick, lifted the branch.

They saw not one, but two, nuggets of gold, cut into two equal parts by the woodsman's axe.

Schönfelde, 14.06.2020

12

THE SEASHELL

One day, the same as every day, a wealthy merchant went to town to see to his business. As he came to the old city gate, he saw a young man sitting amongst the beggars. The merchant was accustomed to stop and give some coins or sweet cakes to the poor, most of whom he knew by name. He was surprised to see the young man, a stranger to him, sitting there with the beggars. He was also a little surprised when he saw that the young man had a sea shell in his hands to which he seemed to be talking. The merchant's interest was piqued, and so he went over to speak to the stranger. As he came closer, he could hear that young man was saying the very nicest of words to the shell.

"My man, why do you speak so to that shell which you hold so gently in your hands?"

"This shell is the shell which holds all of the riches I need within it."

"In what way?"

"All I have to do is ask for a hundred gold coins, and it will get them for me."

"Surely not. Such a thing is not possible."

"Oh, indeed it is. Have you not heard of the gold gathering shell?"

"I have not, I must admit."

"Well, now you have, and now you see one, but leave me alone now while I appreciate what it will do for me. I am waiting for the right moment to receive my gold."

The merchant left the young man to carry on with his adoration of the seashell.

But as he went about his day's work, he could not stop thinking about the shell. How marvellous it would be, he thought, if he could get such riches without having to work for them. If only he had such a sea shell. Before the day was over, he determined to get the young man to sell it to him.

He was most relieved to see the young man still sitting by the city gate amongst the beggars. Still whispering to the shell.

"Tell me," said the merchant, "how much do you want for that shell?"

"Oh. I have never thought about it. You see, I have only just come into possession of it. I have yet to use it. I am still preparing myself to ask it as you see."

"Would you consider selling it to me?"

The young man thought about this for a while. "If I did sell it to you then you would have to give me a hundred coins of course..."

The merchant was pragmatic enough to see sense in this and agreed. He handed over the gold coins and took the seashell home with him. Whereupon he cradled it in his hands and began to say the sweetest words that he could think of saying. Then he started saying some not so lovely things. He was still sitting with the shell in his hands when the cockerel outside crowed to tell the world that it was morning. By this time he had become angry.

At the city gate, he asked where the young man might be found, and a beggar pointed him to the tea shop. He found the object of his anger drinking herbal tea quietly in the corner.

"You tricked me. You have lied and cheated."

"How so?"

"You told me that that seashell would give you a hundred gold coins. And I believed you!"

"But I did not lie and I did not cheat you. The seashell did bring me a hundred gold coins. Your gold coins."

The merchant sat down at the table and regarded the young
man with respect.

"How foolish I am."

"No, how foolish you have been."

Schönfelde, 05.03.2020

13

THE SADHU

This is an Indian tale, but unfortunately, I cannot recall precisely where I found it, or rather, found them, because I read a few versions each with subtle but significant differences in them. I do remember being aware that it had clearly been Westernized.

Over the years of my telling it, it has grown, and particularly the three protagonists have become more clearly defined. While telling stories, I look to understand the underlying meanings of them, and I let them lead me on the journey. For example, in all of the versions, the main man was referred to as a beggar which conjures up images in European minds that are not the ones that people in India hundreds of years ago would have seen. The meaning of a beggar to a listener in the West is not anywhere close to that of one in the East. When I saw him as a mendicant or a yogi, a Sadhu, the dynamics of the story changed considerably. As did his relationship to the other characters and that must consequentially affect his and their actions.

So dear reader, please read on and find out more. [1]

There was once a King who ruled a land in the cold north. He was a hard man with an iron will, and rather than loving him, his people feared him.

Not only was he obstinate, but also he was cruel. He would think nothing of punishing those who offended him by taking their lives, and he relished thinking up unusual ways of doing so.

One day he took a walk with his dog along the shore of the lake upon which he had built his palace. It was early winter, and there were already small patches of ice forming on the surface of the water of the lake.

He walked along throwing a stick which his dog, with a yelp and a wag of the tail, would run off to retrieve. The King liked to do this. It seemed so pointless an activity to him, which made a change from all the business he had to attend to as the King of a great country. As he came nearer to the lake, he cast the stick into the water, but the dog, instead of jumping in after it as he usually did, stood barking out towards the spot where the stick had landed. Her master caught up with the dog and urged her to go in. But each time she put a paw in the water, she pulled back from the edge and just stood there whining. The King wondered why this was. Maybe the water was too cold. He took off one of his boots and dipped his foot into the water, which he swiftly removed. It was indeed very, very cold. So the stick remained where it was, and he and his dog returned to the palace.

That evening, as he sat by the fire looking out across the lake, he began to wonder about just how cold the water might be. And how had the dog known that it would be too cold to enter? How long would she have survived for had she have jumped in? These questions kept him awake long into the night until he decided that he had to find the answers. He was a King and therefore must know everything.

How could he find out? He could just get a slave perhaps, or a prisoner, and throw them into the water. Such was the cruelty of his mind. But that just seemed too easy. No, he felt that there was a bit of pleasure to be had in this. He had an idea.

The next day large notices appeared all around the country and in every town, stating that the King was staging a contest. A challenge. Anybody who could spend twenty-four hours standing up their necks in the water of the lake without any aid to keep them warm as they did so would gain whatever they should ask of him. As the King knew very well that no human being could survive for that long in the nearly frozen lake, he was convinced that he would not have to honour his part of the bargain. Thus he would find out how long a body could survive in the water.

The challenge would take place a week later.

Many young men came. Some were poor, others wealthy. Some were idle and in search of quick riches, while others were simple-minded but brave. The townspeople gathered at the lakeside in front of the palace to observe the spectacle.

The King positioned himself on a balcony to follow the proceedings, and one by one, the hopeful and foolhardy men went down to the lake. They stripped off and stepped into the water, then waded out until they were up to their necks in the lake. Some managed to remain in the water for twenty minutes or so until, half-frozen, they were dragged out by the ropes tied to their ankles. But most gave up after just a few minutes. The King, though entertained by the spectacle, was disappointed with the results.

The day drew on. Then, when most of the crowd had left, a young Sadhu appeared at the lakeside. He bowed to the King and announced that he would be able to stay in the water for as long as the King had stated on his notices. The man was so thin and looked so weak that the King could not imagine that he would succeed. He waved a hand to the young man and told him to try, but he should not forget that he was allowed nothing to keep him warm.

Showing no expression, the Sadhu stepped into the lake. He went out to where the water was deep enough to cover his shoulders and stood very still. He appeared serene and peaceful as he stared up at the balcony where the King sat. An hour later, this expression had not changed. He was used to hardship and well trained in discipline. He knew how to slow his heartbeat down, so his breathing became almost imperceptible. The King watched him ever more intently.

Evening came, and darkness began to fall. Still, the young man calmly stood in the water, his face wearing the same appearance of composure. His eyes stared up to where the King was sitting, even though he could no longer see him clearly for, although the sky was clear and the moon was full, the King was sitting in the shadows. But the King could see the young Sadhu very clearly and began to wonder about how long he could stay there. The night would be a long one.

He retreated further into his mind, further into self. The temperature of the water dropped, but as the fall was gradual, it made no difference to him. He slowed his heartbeat, and time became irrelevant. His existence was now purely in his mind, detached from the lake, the King and his challenge. He was no more aware of these things than he was of the small chunks of ice that were beginning to form on the lake around him. He stared into the hidden distance without blinking, focused solely on the King's balcony and on renouncing pain. His eyes were all that remained of him connected to the world.

His mind, like his body, was being profoundly tested. And the water was getting colder still.

Then a block of ice nudged his shoulder. His focus broke, and he pulled away from self and back into the world. He shuddered as he felt his body.

At the same moment, a small, flickering light appeared at the window next to the King's balcony. The Sadhu's eyes turned toward it. In the glow of a candle, he saw a face. It was that of the King's daughter. She, like her father, had been following the ordeal of the young man in the water.

She had lit a candle to show him that he was not alone.

When he became aware that she was there, he saw compassion in her face. He understood that she would remain at the window as long he endured the freezing lake. She was willing him to stay alive.

His self-control returned, and instead of weakening, he grew stronger. As he stared into the bloom of the candle, he regained control of his mind.

When morning came, he was still alive and still standing up to his chin in the near-frozen water. The stipulated time had passed. As the guards pulled him out, the young man was barely able to move. They to carried him up to the palace. The King heard the crowd, which had returned to witness this marvellous feat, cheering for the Sadhu and he realised that he would now have to keep his part of the bargain. What would the young man ask of him?

The King began to think of ways to get out of the arrangement.

The King's servants wrapped the young man in blankets, and after a few hours, they put him near a small fire. Towards evening, he was able to move and even to speak. The King, begrudgingly, praised him and enquired as to how he had succeeded in staying alive.

The Sadhu explained about the techniques of breathing and the importance of discipline, how he had learnt the mastery of body and mind. He told the King how at the moment he was beginning to lose that control a candle flame had appeared on the window ledge. But he was allowed to speak no further. The King clapped his hands together and shouted out.

"Hah! There was a candle! I told you that you could not have anything to warm you. A candle, its flame must have kept you warm. You have broken the agreement!"

Relieved to have found a way to get out of the bargain he gave the Sadhu no further chance to respond and ordered the palace guards to throw him into the prison.

Thus the King was spared having to reward the poor Sadhu with any of his wealth.

Some days later, the King was sitting at his breakfast table. He saw that his daughter had not joined him and he asked the servants why this was, but none of them could answer him. Nobody had seen her for a while.

When she did not appear that evening, the King began to get concerned. He went to her rooms, but she was not there. He began to worry.

The following morning he took his horse and began to search for her. He searched the coast and rode up into the mountains. He explored every path, stopping in all the villages along the way to search the houses. Wherever he went, he asked about her, but nobody could answer his questions. His searching took him the length and breadth of his lands. In daylight he rode, and at night he slept on the ground beside his horse. Finally, after more than a week of searching and despairing, he gave up and turned his horse in the direction of home.

It was late when, entering the wood that surrounded the palace, he saw a light at the side of the road. He stopped his horse and got down to take a closer look. He pushed his way through the bushes and came into a clearing.

She was sitting on the ground beneath a tall tree staring into a candle.

"Where have you been?"

"Here, father, I have been sitting here."

"You have been missing for more than a week, where have you slept?"

She pointed to a pile of leaves.

"You are a Princess, and you must be looked after and fed. You must come back with me now."

"I cannot, father, I am waiting for my rice to cook."

She pointed up to the top of the tree where the King could see a cooking pot hanging from the uppermost branch.

"But how can you cook rice in a pot hanging in a tree?"

"With the flame of this candle, father."

"How ridiculous you are, daughter! You cannot cook a pot of rice with the flame of a candle. It would not even warm it up from down here."

"But father, you said that it was the flame of a candle that had kept the man in the lake warm. If that is so, as you say, then this candle flame can warm the rice in my pot."

The King felt a chill reach inside his heart as he realised what she had done. She had shown him how heartless he was. She had held up a mirror to him, and he saw brutality. The kindness of her spirit put him to shame.

He blew out the flame of the candle and led her to his horse.

When they returned to the palace, he ordered the guards to fetch the Sadhu from the prison.

When the young man stood before him, it was the King who bowed. Then he spoke words that he had never used before in his life.

"I have maltreated, and I am sorry. Please, I beg your forgiveness and if you grant me that I will grant you anything you wish. Anything that lies within my power."

While in the water staring into the face of the Princess, yet not knowing who she was, he had seen kindness. It was her humanity that had kept him alive. He had understood then, and again later alone in his cell, how much unquestioning compassion for others matters. This recognition had given him a more profound and greater strength of purpose and mind.

The Sadhu forgave the King.

The Princess knew that compassion was not merely pity for someone, but an awareness of their situation, knowledge which demanded action. Her actions had shown her father the injustice of his. The King would change his ways and become a better man because of this.

And what did the Sadhu wish of the King? He asked for a room in which to sleep and a place of peace where he could continue his meditations. The King granted him this.

Through love, the princess had saved the life of the Sadhu and changed that of her father. She remained happy for the rest of her life.

The Sadhu lived in the palace until he died.

Schönfelde, 23.03.2017

---

1. This story first appeared in The Wild Word in 2017. https://thewildword.com/artist-residence-christian-rogers/

14
SIGHT OF HAPPINESS

I have heard this twice. Both times were just in brief tellings. In other words, short and lacking in detail. The first time was from an acquaintance of the road, a traveller, a long time ago, in France. The second was as Jean Reno's character told an uncannily similar, but modernized version about a man that he and Roberto Begnini were about to meet in the film La Tigre e La Neve. Both times I was deeply moved. I have, once again, developed it and given the characters a little more life. I feel that the story has no less of an impact because of this. I have yet to encounter a more touching story of true love than this.

Once there lived a happy man who grew flowers. His contentment came from his work and the lovely woman with whom he shared his life. They had known each other since they were young and had always been the best of friends.

When his day's work was over, he cleaned his tools in the nearby stream, selected the most beautiful flower of those that he grew and carried it home to where his wife awaited him. Its delicate petals nestled in his work-hardened hand.

When she heard him coming - he always kicked his boots off before he came in - she smiled. She could see already, in her mind, the flower he had for her because he brought her one every day.

If she weren't sitting at the table preparing vegetables or at the sink rinsing her dustcloths, then she would be in the garden selecting herbs. Wherever she was and whatever she was doing, he came to her with a single perfect flower which went into her hair.

Their life was simple and satisfied them.

The herbs she grew she would sell on the market once a week. He tended his field every day apart from the one on which he took his flowers to the same market. He had a separate table next to hers. They looked forward to this day more than any other. It was at those tables that they had met. Many years had passed since then, and they had grown together to become happier than they could ever have imagined.

One day that happiness shattered.

She fell ill. The sickness that grew inside her was a mystery, and it gave her much pain. She became so thin and danger-ously weakened that her husband became concerned for her life. He did not leave their house for a single day and was always on hand if she asked anything of him.

However, the illness did not take her, and one day it was gone. But it left scars.

One day she caught sight of her reflection in the window glass. Her skin had parched and withered. And it was in her face, more than anywhere else, that this was evident. She saw that her beauty was gone and that now she resembled someone of more than twice her age.

She took to covering her face with a veil whenever she went out, or if anyone visited. The constant questioning looks troubled her and the sympathetic ones even more so. So she stopped going out or welcoming visitors. In her shame, she would not let even her husband see her face. She recoiled away from him whenever he tried to comfort her. A distance grew between them.

Her spirit seemed broken. She became depressed.

His heart ached to see her distress. Worse still was the hurt he felt being unable to help her.

Then one day, he too began to feel ill. He complained of sharp pains in his head and particularly behind his eyes, and he became dizzy and unstable on his feet. He was told to rest. Doctors came but unable to understand the symptoms they could not find a cure. There was nothing anyone could do. One morning he explained to his wife that his eyesight was getting dim. He became quiet and lethargic. Then one day he turned completely blind.

He became dependent on her. He asked her to help him dress in the mornings and undress at night. She cooked and fed him. After a week or so, she had grown used to her new role and began to forget her misfortune. She would often sit with him and tell him stories. Realizing that he could not see her flawed face, she no longer felt the need for the veil. With him, at least, she was free.

If he complained of boredom, she took him for a walk. In the beginning, they went to his field, but he would ask her how it was, and she had no heart to tell him the truth which was that it was as lost without him as he was without it. One day he suggested she accompanied him to the village. She was hesitant, but then she saw passers-by, uncertain how to react at seeing the blind man and the whithered wife, averting their eyes when they came, and she began to relax. Soon the villagers began to ignore them, overlooking their very existence. They walked every day, and always she described the path they were on and whatever she saw, knowing that it delighted him. Thus she found anew, the beauty of the world. And with that, she rediscovered the pleasure of being in it.

Theirs was unconditional love, for which each was genuinely grateful. Inseparable, their days were slow and tranquil. They lived in harmony and grew old.

She left first, his hand in hers.

As her last breath faded and her eyes closed, in peace, he lowered his head and saw the smile that he had first seen at the market when she had sold her herbs.

Moulay Bouzarqtune, 13.01.2020

15

WINDING PATHS

R oads, like a piece a string, are as long as you make them.

Some are easy to travel along, others are less so. But it is said that a road can be made short if one finds good company. A journey shared is a journey halved.

One morning in the sunshine, two travellers met at a dusty crossing somewhere between the desert and the mountains. After discovering that the journeys that they were taking were to the same city, where they both had their homes, they decided to travel together. As they walked along the lonely road, it became clear that not only were their destinations the same but also their views and philosophies. By the time, a few days later, they reached the journey's end they had become such close friends that they were loathe to part wishing instead to continue the journey together, if not on the road then in their discussions. So it was that they chose to meet in a tea house every evening to continue to debate the matters that were of importance to them.

Each returned to their respective homes and began to think why meeting one another had been of such significance. Both of them being of a philosophical persuasion, this question soon became a point of discussion. The substance of which soon turned to the meaning of friendship.

Their views on what constituted friendship and its worth to them were clear. But neither could find the exact words to give weight to a definition as to what it actually was. They were able to quote philosophers of the past who had compared it to a wine that improves as it matures. Or that having a good friend is like having a blanket on a cold night. But while such maxims seemed to quantify friendship, none shed any light on a deeper meaning.

They decided that there must be a secret to friendship and that together they would search for it.

They spent hours each day discussing matters of more and less import while walking around the city gardens. When one went to the library, the other would keep them company. They shared the books and sometimes even sat next to one another, pouring over the same book. It wasn't long before their undertaking led them to spend entire evenings in each other's society. They shared the preparation of food and its cooking. After meals, they would talk about the day passed and the day to come. Soon they were living entirely in one another's company, alternating between dwellings where one would sleep in a bed, and the other would lay down on the floor nearby.

All the time, they searched for the secret to friendship.

They even travelled together, journeying far and wide as the fancy took them, often going to places that alone neither would have visited. They saw many things and learnt much, but they never felt that either of them had discovered the secret that they sought.

. . .

The years passed slowly and in serenity. The companions grew old and became tired.

One morning in the sunshine, two travellers sat in a garden discussing friendship.

Quietly one spoke while the other listened.

"I wonder when it was that we found the secret?"

"I don't remember."

"Winding paths do not lead to solitude."

Essaouira, 23.01.20

16

THE FIELD

E arly one spring morning, a lone man with a full bag of
seed hanging from his shoulder walked to a field.

The seeds were the seeds of flowers which, in the summer
when they would bloom, he would cut and take to the market
to sell.

As he walked along, he thought about the joy his flowers
would bring when people saw them on the marketplace and
eventually, perhaps, in their homes. The notion that he was
making his living by growing and then trading something that
would give pleasure to people was a good one.

But he was not banking his harvest before it was it gathered.
He knew there was work to do.

When he came to the field, he put the bag of seeds down and,
after stretching and straightening his back to loosen its bones,
he stood quite still, absorbing the scene around him.

To his left, there were the smaller and weaker trees that
marked the beginning of a deep wood. Many wild animals
lived there, and occasionally deer would come to graze on the
grass that grew along the border of the field. Wild boar came
as well, but he knew that neither they nor the deer would
damage the flowers for they could not eat them. Nor would
they trample them because the path they used for their
wanderings ran elsewhere.

He walked along beside the field, occasionally stopping to listen to the silence of the trees.

He came to the far side where there was an open and permanently cultivated stretch of land. For many years it had been overworked, and the soil was pale and dusty, prone to being whipped up by winds that blew in from the East. This land belonged to a farmer whose intention was to suck as much profit out of it as possible. The summer and winter crops were the same every year, and there were always ragged-looking men working at them, no matter the weather. They planted, weeded and gathered, bowed to the ground like the cranes that came in the winter looking for leftovers from the corn harvest. He saw that a group of labourers was there now, silently scraping the earth. It seemed that neither they nor the field would have time to rest.

The flower grower moved on, past stacks of wooden crates. There were others, broken, green and mouldy, that had been thrown into a pile and left to disintegrate.

At the end of the lane that separated the fields, he came to a river. It was low, slow and ponderous and not very wide. Now it was calm and quiet, but there were occasions when it was not, when the snowmelt from the mountains powered its flow, and then it raged, frequently causing damage to the lands through which it travelled. But, in the summer months, it often came close to drying up.

The flower grower waved his hand through the cold clear water to gauge its strength.

The fourth side of the field adjoined a barren wasteland. No-one knew who it was owned by, and it had become a dumping ground, a graveyard for defective wheels, carriage axles and other cast out bits of machinery. Odd shoes and old clothes were rotting amongst scores of cracked or shattered bottles and twisted, misshapen pots and pans that even the tinkers would not touch. Over the years, by burying it all under a shroud of nettles and briar, nature had hidden most of the junk from sight. In the summer months with an intoxicating smell of flowering weeds, the site had gained a beauty of its own. As a dump, it had remained unwanted, but nature, left to its own devices, had reclaimed it.

He returned to the place from where he had started, and he looked to the field. Situated within a wood, a stretch of dreary exhausted earth, the river and a dump, was the place he chose to work to improve not only his life but also those of others by planting beautiful things and providing them with a place to thrive.

Next to him were the seeds of his endeavour, in the bag on the ground at his feet. They were all that he needed.

The year before, as the autumn rain clouds had begun to gather depth and the days to shorten, he had cleared away the faded stalks of the previous crop and lightly tilled the earth so that the winter's frost could penetrate and break up the soil. He understood how nature would work for him if he allowed it. Sometimes, during the winter months, he had come to look at his field and touch the earth, so that he could feel its pulse.

As the impending arrival of spring had become more evident through the birdsong and the sight of early buds around him, he had begun to plan the sowing for he knew it would be foolish to waste the seeds, and he was a prudent man.

Now he stood to assess the condition of the field.

Near the forest, where, over many seasons, the leaves had fallen, he knew the earth to be richer in nutrients. But also, he knew that as they had decomposed, the leaves had turned the soil slightly more acidic. This meant that the earth there would be harsher on the seeds and less welcoming to the developing plants even though the flowers that would eventually grow there might have gained strength from the struggle.

He also considered the shadows the trees would cast. There would be less sunlight to nourish the flowers, but the shade would be advantageous to them in a time of drought.

As always with nature, there were two sides to her character.

The field had a slight inclination leading down to the bank along which the river ran. There the flowers would not need so much watering. The moisture from the early rising mist would see to that.

He figured that the part of the field that edged onto the wasteland and the unsightly litter of human waste and rusting metal was at risk. The flowers there would need some sort of protection against exposure to any contamination which might hamper their growth.

When he had finished surveying the field, had covered every aspect of its state and calculated every eventuality, he was fully aware of the extent of the task before him.

He bent his knee to the ground and focussed his attention to the soil. It was warming. Carefully he examined it, not just with his eyes but also with his fingers, which understood. He sifted it in the way that a miller might in reckoning the strength of his flour. Then he picked up his sack and prepared to sow the seeds.

He softly scooped fistfuls of seed from within the bag and with deliberate movements, he cast them about him. As he walked, he scanned the ground ahead of him. He worked with purpose.

Whenever he found a hard clod of earth, he would gently prise it open, and softly, crumble it back into the soil again. When he came across cracks where the surface had dried, he closed them with his fingers, filling them in with soil from nearby. If he discovered stones, he chucked them out to the edge of the field. Later, he would gather them and add to the piles of the ones he had already removed. These would become a low wall by the waste tip. Occasionally, he found discarded bits of twine which had blown down from the industrial farmland. These he kept and used.

When he had emptied his sack of the seeds, he left the field and walked home.

His thoughts remained with the field. Every few days, he went back to there to look for the sprouting seedlings and, when he saw them, to check their progress. But his concern was not only for the young plants. Indeed, it was more for the earth and the environment into which he had sown them.

In some parts, he saw that the rain was able to seep deep enough into the soil, to the delicate roots, but there were others where it did not sink in at all. There, he carved little channels in the ground in which the water could flow and gather where it was needed most. He never considered the value of one section of the field to be more or less than another in his mind, the whole of the land deserved the same care and attention. It was his calling to look after it, and he took this responsibility very seriously.

The seedlings grew tall and filled out. They became vigorous, wholesome and took on identities of their own. The field became a field of flowers.

Now, he went there each day. How beautiful the colours were which mirrored the brilliance of the sun that had nourished them. Their beauty pleased him. He knew that the seeds he had sown had been good one's and the conditions had been favourable. But the highest satisfaction came in seeing that the soil was supporting the crop and, of course, knowing that his work had been productive.

He gave names to the flowers whose colours became poems to him. Blue ones he called "Smiling Sky". The orange ones became "Daughters of the Sun". His favourites, although he tried to suppress such an idea, were white with pale hints of pink. These he called "Mothers of the World."

These were names that he would never tell anyone. Such poetry was for him alone. But he did hope that others would find their own names for them.

He worked happily amongst the flowers supporting the weaker ones with canes and thinning out those that needed to be. But even as he caressed the flowers and his fingers searched out brown leaves or broken heads, his thoughts never strayed from the field or the space around it. He took pains to remove any windblown rubbish he found. He decided that between the wasteland and the field, he would encourage a hedge to grow over the stones that he had put there. The hedge would encourage birds to come and build nests and they would then take bugs and moths from the flowers to feed their young. Perhaps he would grow a hedge that would bear fruit.

He cared for the river by clearing its banks and removing anything that did not belong there. By doing this, the flow remained steady and regular, lessening the danger of the river spilling into the field. It also ensured the water was clean enough for him to use for watering.

Sometimes, as he watched the careless and unfulfilled workers nearby, stooped to their tasks, he imagined closing off his field to protect it against, what he saw as, the foolishness outside.

The flowers were healthy. Some were now ready to be picked and taken to the market.

He didn't gather the flowers all at once but went each day to fill a wicker pannier which, when full, he carried on his back as he took the path along the river to town. He sold them in small and large bunches to rich and poor people alike but never for a fixed price. As often as not, he was happy to accept whatever he was offered, and sometimes it was just a smile.

With the money he bought supplies, things he would need for the winter and he was careful to leave enough to put by for seed for the following years.

When summer was over and the colder days came, he would gather up the bamboo canes, tie them into bundles which he would take home with him. There he would repair the bucket, straighten the tines on his fork and shake away the dry earth from the empty seed sack. The mornings would come when he could sleep longer without the need to get up with the sun to tend to the flowers, and then he would be happy to read and drink tea in the quiet of his house.

In autumn, when the trees were bare, and the empty bird nests could be seen silhouetted in the solid white sky, he would return to the field with his fork and fold the earth lightly in on itself. Any fallen branches or sticks he found he would take to the side of the field to be a part of the hedge he was creating.

But for now, as he stood viewing his grown-up flowers, he saw the work he had done. And that he had done it well.

In return for his stewardship of the field and the soil, he had received the blessing of beauty. And of seeing the joy of others.

He was already thinking about the dark days of winter. He would come to the field once in a while. Just see if it was still alright.

Schönfelde, 04.11.2018

17

THE RIVER

There was once a man who looked out of his window rarely seeing what was beyond it.

He was a simple man, but his wits were not dim.

There had been no significant transitions in his life because he had not sought any.

One morning the sky turned leaden, and there followed many days of falling rain. When the flooding began, the owners of the other houses in the lane were forced to construct defences against the waters that flowed in front of their doors. The man, whose home was higher up than the others, stood on his doorstep and watched them. He became aware of the intensity of the water. He sensed that it had come from afar and that it would travel still further.

Not knowing why he stepped out and into the stream. He was barefoot, and he could feel the pressure of the flow on his ankles. This exhilarated him.

Urged on, his steps took direction from the thrust of the water. To not lose his balance, he could not look back.

The river of rainfall following the route of least resistance, wended between two lightly wooded hills and across a field of ripe wheat, until it came to a ravine, into which it fell to join what was now a gushing, bubbling river.

The man stood and looked down astonished at seeing this because what was usually just a small stream, which rose near to his house, was now a considerable torrent. He wondered what all that energy could do, where it would go.

He climbed down the bank and let himself slip into the water.

It was not cold, but the pressure forced him to take deeper breaths.

The wider the river became, the slower and less insistent the water seemed. He was floating now and needed no effort to stay that way. He lay on his back and looked up to the sky. His eyes beheld the clouds, which were now soft and white. He saw stretches of blue between them in which the sun sometimes appeared. Its rays warmed his face. As he drifted along, weightless, his head bobbing above the surface of the water, he was aware of every oscillation and undercurrent. His movements, like his reflexes, were of little consequence. No longer able to influence the situation or his direction. He was free from the burden of choice.

Experiencing the river from within rather than from its banks was strange. Perspective and shapes shifted as he observed everything from below. The trees, now taller, more slender, gained stature, and houses, those close to the bank's edge, became more imposing. Everything he saw had increased in magnitude. Passing underneath the bridges, their arches dappled by a reflected light giving them their own sky, they seemed larger from below than they had ever been from above.

Hidden places were no longer hidden. He noticed cobwebs glistening in the sunshine which were strung between the branches of dead trees and, again below the corbel arch of a footbridge enmeshed in abandoned straw built nests which had never known rain. Passing through a village, he saw the rubbish heaps that spilt into the river from the back ends of gardens. He saw broken algae-coated furniture which had been dumped in the river that now lay peacefully at rest in watery graves just below the surface. Further downstream, a flock of adventurous starlings rose from a field and flew over-head. For a while, oblivious of his presence, a single swift accompanied him. Sweeping along, it grabbed the insects that skated on the surface of the water.

He wept with pleasure at this.

Habituated to the laws of the water, he slept for short spells while the river, which kept him away from the snagging banks, carried him along. Time, like the river, became immea-surable. His body adjusted and cooled to the temperature of the water, and his heartbeat followed its rhythm.

Later, on the third day, the sky turned grey, and a light rain fell for an hour or so. He saw how round raindrops were. He tried to discern if the droplets that bounced back up were the raindrops themselves or the water it was displacing. For a while, a soft white mist lingered over the surface of the water-way, hiding him from sight. With it, he was truly absorbed into the river.

He was water now. He had become the river.

As it flowed along, the river did not gather strength, which waned, but volume.

Other tributaries joined in, bringing waters which came from further away. Waters which had different attitudes and dispositions. Through the knowledge conveyed to it by these smaller rivers, which it relentlessly swallowed up, the river grew in wisdom. Those that had flowed down from the mountains were as cool as the snow that they had been. While others whose journeys had been across vast grassy plains were opaque and weedy. Some were merely streams, yet they carried memories of the mighty winds of the steppe or the subtle breezes of the forests. Such waters had passed through desert sands, had fallen in tall cascading waterfalls or had meandered through the roots of plants and magnificent trees.

These secondary sources flowed from mouths which contributed to rather than fed from the river. A river which accepted all that it was offered.

But soon it began to allow small rivers to branch away from the main body. These were mouths that needed feeding fresh, unpolluted water which, by irrigating crops in fields or by flowing into greater or smaller lakes, some pure others stagnant, would encourage and support life. Even to brackish marshes where swarms of insects provided food for birds and bats.

Wherever the water went, it would make a difference.

To suit its purpose, while inexorably following a course toward a destination decided long ago, the river's form continuously changed. At times, passing through treeless plains, it was unhurried at others in sharp rock-split ravines, its movements became erratic and intense. Passing beneath castellated shadows of old town walls, it was sluggish but respectful in allowing and following their guidance. It was as capable of crashing through a rockfall as it was of slipping gently, quietly over a sandy bank. It mattered very little what it encountered or through which landscape it flowed. Its purpose was undeniable.

Then came a time of near silence. The surface of the water seemed like that of a vast sheet of ice, shifting only slightly. Odd and occasional swirling pockets of ripples rising to the surface were all that broke the illusion. The whole body of water moved as one. Its behaviour was no longer influenced by the landscape which contained it for it was the landscape— a waterscape. From the middle of the barely moving river, the banks on either side were scarcely visible, and, at times, apart from a solitary tree or a raised landmass, there was nothing to indicate land of any sort. There was only water.

He heard voices.

They were distant, coming to him, rolling across the surface of the water, borne on a breeze from far away.

They spoke only to him and were persistent, urgent.

He became aware that his feet were dragging. The riverbed was soft and acquiescent.

For the first time since stepping into the flooding river, he stood still. As still as the gentle flow which caressed and pressed his back would allow. He felt the current eddying around his legs, his waist. But they no longer urged him on for this was as far as they would take him.

There was another force ahead before which even the river must bow.

He had no understanding of the time he had spent in the river. Or of how far he had travelled. Nor did he seek it. He was here, and this was now.

Where he knew he should be.

The waves called to him.

Their call was not a command.

It was advice to sit and be calm.

He walked to the edge of the sea and felt the flux and reflux of gentle waves lapping his feet. He stayed like this for a while, thinking about his self. Then he turned and walked along the beach until he spotted a dry sandy hill to sit on.

From there, he looked out at the vastness of an ocean.

An ocean of stories.

Schönfelde, 20.06.2020

18

THE AFTERWORDS

I hope that these stories have informed, entertained and delighted. That is their intention.

Apart from The River, The Field and The Seller Of Words, I am not the owner or the author of these tales, and nor do I wish to be thought as being such. Older versions of them are all in the public domain and belong to no one person. Therefore I neither claim nor hold copyright on them, except for the three above mention tales.

The illustrations, however, are under copyright in the name of Christian Wingrove-Rogers.